TEMPTED & TAMED

...by two red-hot men!

Meeting the hottest guys in town
changes the lives of sisters
Scarlett and Ruby Anderson for ever!

When sensible Scarlett is tempted by sinfully
sexy Jake—a doctor by day and a *sinner*
by night!—their one night of passion has
consequences that will last a lifetime…

And rebellious Ruby finally finds a reason to
stick around as deliciously hot racing car driver
Noah becomes the only man to tame her!

Be tempted and tamed by these red-hot heroes
in Emily Forbes's delectable duet:

A DOCTOR BY DAY…

and

TAMED BY THE RENEGADE

Both titles are available now!

Dear Reader

I'd like to introduce you to the Anderson sisters—Scarlett, Ruby and Rose—and their search for a happily-ever-after. Scarlett doesn't think she needs one, Ruby doesn't think she deserves one, and Rose looks as if she might not get one. But all that is about to change...

In A DOCTOR BY DAY... Scarlett—the rational, clever, eldest sister—is swept off her feet by Jake, a sexy younger man with an unconventional part-time job, who upends her orderly world and steals her heart. And in TAMED BY THE RENEGADE Ruby, the rebellious middle sister, falls in love for the first time when gorgeous Noah gets under her defences and teaches her how to love and accept—not only him, but also herself.

These two Anderson sisters might not have a lot in common, but I discovered they both have a thing for good-looking bare-chested men and, as usual, I had fun creating the heroes for my heroines. Jake and Noah are strong and loyal, smart and sexy, with slight non-conformist streaks—perfect for Scarlett and Ruby, even if they take some convincing.

I hope you enjoy these first two stories. I haven't decided if I'll give Rose her own story yet—she's putting up a good case for it in my imagination, but I'm tempted to let you decide. If you'd like to read about Rose I'd love to hear from you. Drop me a line at emilyforbes@internode.on.net

Until then, happy reading

Emily

***Emily Forbes won a
2013 Australia Romantic Book of the Year Award
for her title
SYDNEY HARBOUR HOSPITAL: BELLA'S WISHLIST.***

TAMED BY
THE RENEGADE

BY
EMILY FORBES

MILLS
BOON

First published in Great Britain 2014
by Mills & Boon, an imprint of Harlequin (UK) Limited,
Eton House, 18-24 Paradise Road, Richmond, Surrey, TW9 1SR

© 2014 Emily Forbes

ISBN: 978-0-263-24401-4

are natural,
od grown in
ocesses conform
f origin.

Emily Forbes began her writing life as a partnership between two sisters who are both passionate bibliophiles. As a team, 'Emily' had ten books published. One of her proudest moments was winning the 2013 Australia Romantic Book of the Year Award for SYDNEY HARBOUR HOSPITAL: BELLA'S WISHLIST.

While Emily's love of writing remains as strong as ever, the demands of life with young families have recently made it difficult to work on stories together. But rather than give up her dream Emily now writes solo. The challenges may be different, but the reward of having a book published is still as sweet as ever.

Whether as a team or as an individual, Emily hopes to keep bringing stories to her readers. Her inspiration comes from everywhere, and stories she hears while travelling, at mothers' lunches, in the media and in her other career as a physiotherapist all get embellished with a large dose of imagination until they develop a life of their own.

If you would like to get in touch with Emily you can e-mail her at emilyforbes@internode.on.net

Recent titles by Emily Forbes:

THE HONOURABLE ARMY DOC
DARE SHE DATE THE CELEBRITY DOC?
BREAKING THE PLAYBOY'S RULES
SYDNEY HARBOUR HOSPITAL: BELLA'S WISHLIST*
GEORGIE'S BIG GREEK WEDDING?
BREAKING HER NO-DATES RULE
NAVY OFFICER TO FAMILY MAN
DR DROP-DEAD-GORGEOUS
THE PLAYBOY FIREFIGHTER'S PROPOSAL

**Sydney Harbour Hospital*

These books are also available in eBook format from www.millsandboon.co.uk

Dedication

For my fabulous brothers and sisters-in-law:
Andrew, Tim, Michelle, Brigid, Terry, Rebecca, Nick,
Alexandra, Duncan, Nick, Rachel, Luke, Danielle, Ben
and Kiera—with love.

PROLOGUE

Sunday, 14th December

RUBY HAD ALWAYS known she'd have to grow up one day but she'd suspected it would be a gradual process, like growing out a fringe or recovering from a broken heart. She never expected to have to grow up overnight.

A few hours earlier she'd been asleep in her bed. Now she was about to walk into an intensive care unit halfway across the country and she was terrified of what she would find. She didn't know if she was strong enough to deal with this crisis. She suspected she was a flight-not-fight type of personality. In fact, she knew she was. She'd always run away when the going had got tough.

Perhaps being able to cope with traumatic situations was a sure sign of maturation. The trouble was she was afraid of what she was about to see and afraid she wouldn't cope.

Maybe this disaster would be the catalyst that forced her to grow up. Maybe it would trigger her development into the sort of person others could depend on, but she really wasn't sure if she had that level of resolve.

She waited as her sister's fiancé keyed the security

code into the door and held it for her and then she trailed in Jake's footsteps as he crossed the room.

Ruby could see her sister, Scarlett, and their mother sitting side by side. Scarlett was holding their mother's hand and Ruby knew she was comforting Lucy, not the other way around. Scarlett had always looked after all of them, their mother included.

Seeing her family huddled together threatened to damage the wall around the well of emotion that she'd been trying to keep under control since she'd left Byron Bay in the early hours of the morning. Throughout the flight to Adelaide, and even on the short trip from the airport to the hospital, she'd fought to keep her emotions in check. She hadn't wanted to fall apart in front of a plane full of strangers or in front of her sister's fiancé—she didn't know him well enough yet and she couldn't let him see that she wasn't as brave or as strong as Scarlett was.

Scarlett stood up the moment she saw Ruby. She came towards her with her arms open and wrapped Ruby in her embrace. Ruby relaxed into her older sister's comforting hug. She could feel the tears welling in her eyes and gathering on her lashes ready to spill over as she soaked up Scarlett's reassurance.

She and Scarlett were of similar height but Ruby's skinny frame was always a sharp contrast to Scarlett's curves. Even more so today, thought Ruby as she felt Scarlett's rounded belly, firm and hard and stretched tight as a drum, pressing into her. Ruby stepped back out of Scarlett's embrace to take a proper look at her. Scarlett was into the final trimester of her pregnancy and it was the first time Ruby had seen her in several months, the first time she'd seen her looking pregnant. It suited her.

But seeing Scarlett's new curves served as another little push to Ruby's subconscious, another little hint that times were changing and she might have to change along with them. Scarlett had always been there for her. They'd always been close because Scarlett had made that her priority. Their relationship had been nurtured, and on occasion saved, by Scarlett's determination and perseverance. She'd been there for all of them at one time or another but now she had another person totally dependent on her. Her fiancé and their baby would be Scarlett's priorities now.

Ruby knew that didn't mean that Scarlett would abandon any of them. Not her, not their mother and certainly not Rose, their younger sister and the reason they were all here in the ICU, but Scarlett couldn't be expected to shoulder all their worries. Rose needed them and they needed to look out for her. *She* needed to look out for Rose.

She'd never really given much thought to how her family was faring. She'd chosen her own path at the age of sixteen and hadn't spent much time considering others. She realised now how selfish she'd been. It was time for her to step up.

She hugged her mother next. Anyone watching may have thought it strange that she greeted her sister before her mother but Ruby and Lucy didn't have an easy relationship. Ruby had always felt far more comfortable sharing her thoughts and feelings with her sister, but she recognised that the sometimes stilted relationship she had with her mother was her own fault. She'd always pushed her mother away. Ruby had always wanted to assert her independence and it had backfired on her in spectacular fashion during her teenage years but she'd been too proud then to admit her mistakes. She wasn't sure if she'd changed all that much in the ensuing years.

'It's good to have you home.' Lucy welcomed her with open arms.

Her mother would say she was home but Adelaide hadn't been home to Ruby for almost eleven years. She wasn't sure where she would say home was. But she wasn't going to argue over semantics now. It wasn't important. She was going to be mature and agreeable. Whether she called Adelaide home or not was irrelevant—she was here now. A week earlier than planned. She'd had flights booked for the end of the week, scheduled for Scarlett and Jake's wedding, she hadn't planned on making a middle of the night dash to the bedside of her critically ill little sister.

Ruby could hear the soft click and hiss of the ventilator behind her. So far she'd avoided looking at Rose and still she hesitated. She wasn't sure if she could handle seeing her younger sister lying in a hospital bed connected to machines.

She let go of her mother and asked, 'Have the doctors been back? Have they said anything more?' She asked the question even though she was unsure about whether she was ready to hear the answer.

She knew the question was just another delaying tactic. When Jake had met her at the airport he'd told her what they knew about Rose's condition so far. Which wasn't much and not nearly enough to thaw the icy fingers that had gripped her heart since Scarlett had phoned her in the middle of the night. She knew the doctors suspected meningitis and had put Rose into a medically induced coma and started her on a course of antibiotics, but Jake hadn't been able to tell her anything further.

She had directed her question at Scarlett and was struck again how she automatically turned to her sister and not their mother in a crisis. Scarlett, as the eldest of the Anderson sisters, had always been the level-headed one. The one who everyone in their scrambled family turned to in times of crisis, but Ruby had a premonition that this crisis might be too big for Scarlett to handle alone and she suspected she would have to be prepared to stand up and be counted too. The only issue was she didn't know if she was capable of that.

Up until now Ruby had done a very good job of avoiding major responsibility but it seemed times might be changing. She was going to have to be prepared to take some of the burden from Scarlett.

She'd had plenty of experience of her life changing around her without warning or consultation. It had been something that had shaped her into the woman she was today, one who wanted total control over her own life. One who didn't want to give anyone else an opportunity to upset her apple cart. Taking control hadn't always worked out so well for her but at least her mistakes, downfalls and dramas had been of her own making.

But even though recently she'd been doing a relatively good job of controlling her own little world she wasn't able to control the world that existed around her, and the wider world had a habit of intruding when she didn't want it to and throwing curve balls her way.

Scarlett shook her head in reply to Ruby's question. Jake and Scarlett were both doctors yet they had no more insight into Rose's situation and the lack of information frustrated Ruby.

Ruby herself wasn't a stranger to hospitals. All the sights and sounds and smells, which to many others would seem unfamiliar, were nothing unusual for her. She was a nurse, she'd had plenty of experience looking after patients and their families but she'd never been on the other side. She'd never had to sit by and watch while someone she loved was on life support and being cared for by a team of doctors and nurses. It was a very different situation and, for reasons she didn't fully understand yet, it made her uneasy. She knew it was, in part, due to exhaustion. She was tired and emotional but she had to face her fears. She'd been on the go since four this morning and lack of sleep wasn't making things any rosier.

Rose.

She needed to face her fears. She needed to see Rose.

She could feel anxiety gripping her chest, adding to the pressure of those icy fingers around her heart as she forced herself to look at her younger sister. She knew she was nervous, worried about the sight that was going to confront her. She turned to the bed.

Half a dozen various tubes and leads connected Rose to monitors and to life. Ruby tried to ignore the mechanical sounds of the ventilator as she focused on Rose. The pale skin of her arms was covered in a purple rash that was indicative of septicaemia but the rash didn't appear to have spread to her face. Ruby didn't know how she would have reacted to that. Rose had always been unbelievably pretty and Ruby didn't want to face such a stark and obvious sign of Rose's affliction. She looked as though she was sleeping and Ruby was grateful for small mercies.

But she still didn't understand why nothing was happening. Everyone was sitting around, waiting. If the doctors wanted to run more tests, where were they? Why wasn't someone doing something? What were they waiting for?

'Where are the doctors?' She turned away from Rose and, out of habit as much as anything else, once again directed her question to Scarlett. She forced herself to look at Lucy next. Forced herself to include her mother, but Lucy looked as though she was in shock and Ruby doubted she'd even heard her question.

Her mother looked tired. Lucy had always been beautiful. Scarlett had inherited her looks but although Lucy often looked tired, Ruby had never thought she looked older than her years. Until today.

Lucy had been only eighteen when Scarlett was born and they were often mistaken for sisters. But Ruby knew people wouldn't be making that mistake today. Sitting side by side, their similarities were still obvious but so was their age difference. Growing up, Ruby had longed for their colouring, longed for their dark hair, dark eyes and flawless fair skin. She had the fair skin but she'd hated her red hair, even though her mother had insisted it was strawberry blond, and the smattering of freckles that were strewn across the bridge of her nose.

Ruby could see some strands of grey in Lucy's dark hair, which she didn't remember seeing before. She knew she had caused some of the lines on her mother's face but there were more of those too than there used to be. Definitely more than there had been a few months ago when Ruby had last come back to Adelaide, and she suspected the events of the past twelve hours had put them there.

But this wasn't about her or her mother now. It was about Rose, and she needed to stay calm and positive. Biting back a scream of frustration, she looked back at Scarlett, wanting someone to answer her.

'They're waiting for the results of the blood tests,' Scarlett told her.

'I thought they'd diagnosed meningitis?'

Scarlett nodded. 'They're treating her for septicaemia and bacterial meningitis but they haven't identified the strain yet.'

Ruby knew that bacterial meningitis was more serious than the viral form and she also knew that the prognosis varied widely between the different strains of bacteria and between different people. What she didn't understand was how Rose could have caught the disease.

'How did this happen? How did Rose get sick?' As she asked yet another question she wondered if they should be talking in front of Rose. She believed that coma patients could hear conversations going on around them but she figured Rose had probably heard everything else that had been discussed so far this morning.

'No one can really say,' Jake answered, 'but the most likely scenario is that Rose picked it up at work in the after-school care facility. The bacteria can't live outside the body for long so people need to be in close contact.'

Rose was studying to be a primary school teacher and her practical work plus her part-time job in an after-school care facility would give her plenty of exposure to all manner of bugs.

'But it's also reasonably common in young adults aged between fifteen and twenty-four so it's almost impossible to tell where she came into contact with it.' Jake shrugged.

Rose was twenty-one, six years younger than Ruby, and her age put her right inside the high-risk age bracket.

Ruby glanced at Scarlett as a realisation hit her. 'Is it safe for you to be in here?' she asked. Scarlett's pregnancy was definitely showing but Ruby couldn't remember enough about the disease to know if Scarlett was putting herself or her baby at risk.

Scarlett nodded in reply. 'I'm fine. It's passed through sneezing and coughing via droplets in the air.' They both looked at Rose. Attached to the ventilator, she wasn't doing either of those things.

'Has anyone else from the school fallen ill?'

'We haven't been told but anyone she had contact with at school will be given antibiotics as a precaution, but there are other possibilities that complicate things further in terms of treating other people but don't really affect Rose's treatment. What the doctors need to do now is identify the strain of bacterium.'

'Rose was out at a lunch for a friend's birthday yesterday. She came home early and said she wasn't feeling well and went straight to bed.' Lucy added to Jake's tale. 'We assume she was already infected when she went to lunch but because there can be such a short period of time between becoming infected and presenting with symptoms it's adding to the confusion. When she came home she had a temperature and a headache but it didn't seem anything out of the ordinary. She didn't complain about a stiff or sore neck or a rash. I didn't see any of the red flags for meningitis so I just assumed it was a flu virus.'

Lucy was also a nurse but she worked in aged care, and meningitis wasn't something she saw much of.

'She got up to go to the bathroom around midnight and I heard her collapse. When I reached her she was having trouble breathing and that's when I noticed the rash. I rang the ambulance and even though they arrived quickly, by the time we got to the hospital she had gone downhill rapidly. She was in cardiac failure, her blood pressure was too low to register and she had no pulse. The rash on her body was spreading before my eyes. I just wish I'd suspected something more sinister than flu to begin with.'

'I'm not sure that anyone would have, Lucy. You know how variable the signs and symptoms can be and how often they're missed.'

Jake's words were meant to be reassuring but Ruby doubted anything would ease her mother's conscience. Not yet. Not until they knew Rose's prognosis and maybe not even then. But Ruby was grateful to Jake for being there to support them all. She knew Scarlett and Lucy would be struggling with the situation as much as she was and it wasn't fair to expect Scarlett to support them all. They couldn't expect Scarlett to have enough strength for all of them. Not always.

Ruby was pleased that Scarlett now had Jake to take care of her. No one was looking to lean on Ruby but neither was anyone offering a shoulder to support her. She had always rebuffed offers of help or support so she supposed no one thought she might need some now.

Before she could follow that train of thought any further they were interrupted by one of the ICU nurses and a trio of doctors.

'The doctors want to do a lumbar puncture,' the nurse explained.

Four pairs of eyes swivelled to the doctors.

'Now?' Lucy asked.

The doctors were nodding. Ruby wondered who they all were and what they did, but no one seemed to think it was important to introduce her.

'We really need to identify the bacterium responsible for the infection as the outcomes can be vastly different.' The doctor who spoke looked easily the more senior of the three. Balding and carrying some extra weight, Ruby assumed he was the specialist. 'There are increased mortality rates and poorer outcomes with the pneumococcal strain compared to meningococcal. It's fatal in about ten per cent of cases and one in seven will suffer a permanent disability.'

Ruby had heard enough now. She wished he'd stop talking.

'We don't know yet whether there's any permanent damage to her heart and some of her other major organs are showing signs of stress. We're hoping to minimise the damage to her vital organs and her extremities but we need to make a proper diagnosis in order to implement the right treatment.'

Ruby was feeling sick. She didn't want to think about the consequences of Rose's illness. She didn't want to think about what else could go wrong. She wanted to believe that Rose would get better and that everything would go back to normal.

So much for being positive and grown up.

'The next thirty-six to forty-eight hours are critical.'

And Ruby knew immediately what the doctor meant.

Rose had to get through the next two days if she was going to have any chance of surviving.

CHAPTER ONE

EVERYONE ELSE HEARD the unspoken words too and Ruby watched as Scarlett turned to Jake.

It seemed she was right, Scarlett couldn't be expected to support them all. This was one time when she needed someone to support her. Lucy wouldn't be able to lean on Scarlett, she had enough to deal with. Ruby might need to be the one to offer her mother comfort now.

As the medical team began to set up for the lumbar puncture Ruby found herself, along with the rest of her family, being ushered out of Rose's cubicle.

The ICU had suddenly become a hive of activity and Ruby had to stop and wait as another patient was wheeled in and she was separated from the others by the barouche. As the bed was pushed past her she caught a glimpse of a solidly built man and she immediately wondered what had happened to him.

What had brought him to the ICU? There were usually only a couple of reasons why young men ended up here—accidents, usually involving vehicles, or serious illness. She turned her head, watching as he went past. Despite the oxygen mask covering his face, he looked too well to be seriously ill. His face was tanned and his colour was good and the one arm that she could see poking out from under the blankets was also tanned and well muscled. He looked robust and healthy enough.

She could see the outline of a cradle that was keeping the weight of the blankets off his leg and was suggestive of a lower-limb fracture. A motorbike accident, she decided before she ducked around the end of his bed to catch up with Scarlett and their mother.

They were hovering in the corridor, looking lost. They looked unsure what to do as they waited for the doctors to finish with Rose. Ruby was exhausted. It had been a crazy day—emotional, upsetting and stressful. She didn't want to pace the hospital corridors, waiting for Rose's procedure to be completed, she needed a shower and some fresh air to give her some strength to face what was yet to come.

'Does anyone mind if I go and have a shower while the doctors are with Rose?' Ruby asked.

She knew Lucy would wait and she knew Scarlett wouldn't let her wait alone. Ruby also knew that she should offer to stay too. Hadn't she just told herself she would need to be the one to offer support to her mother? But she couldn't do it. She knew she'd go crazy with the tension of waiting and that would inevitably lead to her picking a fight with Lucy, something neither of them needed. She told herself it was best for everyone if she got away from the hospital and cleared her head before she exploded.

'I'll give you a lift to our place, if you like,' Jake offered, when no one insisted she stay.

'Don't you want to wait with Scarlett? There'd be a shower in the hospital I could use, surely?' She knew Scarlett would be able to organise a shower for her in the staff facilities at the hospital but she would prefer to get outside. She really wanted a chance to get some fresh air at the same time.

'It'll be nicer to shower at our house,' Scarlett replied.

'It's only five minutes to home and your bag is still in my car,' Jake said. The two of them were giving her permission to leave and she wasn't going to argue further.

'Are you sure you don't mind ferrying me around?' she asked him, as they left the hospital and returned to his car.

'Not at all. I'm just doing whatever needs to be done at the moment—chauffeur, cook, liaison person.'

'Liaison person?'

'Between your family and the medical team,' he explained. 'It's difficult for Scarlett and your mum to ask the right questions, they're too close. It seems to work best if I do it.'

'How can you do all that and go to work?'

'I was already on holidays leading up to the wedding. I've quit The Coop.'

'You've quit?'

Jake laughed. 'In case you haven't noticed, I'm about to become a husband and a father. I think my nights spent working in a strip club have been numbered for a while. It's time to move on to the more responsible stage of my life. I start my internship in three weeks. Quitting The Coop now was supposed to give us time for a honeymoon. So I am at your service. Anything you need, just ask.'

Ruby appreciated the offer. She had come to think of Jake as the brother she wished she had.

Jake was a good man. It was lucky for Scarlett that when Ruby had met Jake it had been clear he'd only had eyes for Scarlett, otherwise who knew what would have happened? Only Ruby did know, Jake was cute and smart but far too conventional for her. She smiled to herself, not quite believing she would ever describe someone who worked as stripper in a male revue club called The Coop as conventional! In fact, his gig as a stripper was far more in keeping with the type of man she usually looked for. Her men were always a little bit edgy. She needed the excitement. But despite his old job Jake was basically a good person. He wouldn't be able to handle someone like her.

Scarlett was perfect for him. As he was for her. Jake was cute and smart. Scarlett was clever and sensible and they made a good match. Plus it was obvious that he adored her and, most importantly, he allowed Scarlett to be herself instead of the person Scarlett thought she should be or the one she thought people wanted her to be. That had always been Scarlett's undoing. She always wanted to please everybody.

The same thing could definitely *not* be said about *her*.

Jake pulled to a stop in front of Scarlett's renovated cottage. Ruby grabbed her duffel bag from the boot of his dark green MG and followed him through the gate in the high brick wall and into the tiny front garden. She was travelling light, and hadn't had time to do more than throw a change of clothes into her bag before racing to the airport. She had known that the phone call in the early hours of the morning would only be bad news. A phone call in the blackest part of the night was only *ever* bad news.

Now that she was here, she had no recollection of what she'd actually packed. She hoped she had at least one change of clothes, although if she'd forgotten anything she'd borrow it from Scarlett. She had none of Scarlett's curves but, being summer, she'd get away with wearing her sister's clothes. It didn't matter if they were loose on her and in desperate times she knew Scarlett had several tops that could be worn as dresses.

Jake slid his key into the lock on the front door. A Christmas wreath decorated the door, jolting Ruby back to the present. Christmas was less than two weeks away but she had never felt in less of a festive mood.

'You know where everything is,' he said, as he held the door open for her. 'Make yourself at home.'

Ruby always stayed with Scarlett when she visited. It worked best if she and Lucy had their own space, but she hadn't thought about the ramifications of her earlier arrival. She'd originally planned to arrive two days before the wedding, timing her arrival with Jake's temporary move back to his parents' home, but now that she was here early she hadn't considered that a change of plan might be needed.

'Does it still suit you for me to stay? I'm not crowding you?' she asked.

'It's fine,' he assured her. 'The spare bedroom is still yours to use.'

'Are you sure? I can stay at Mum's.' She could manage a few days there if necessary.

'Ruby, don't worry about it. Have a shower and I'll be back to pick you up in about forty minutes, okay?'

She nodded and stopped arguing and pushed open the door to the spare bedroom. She upended her bag on the bed and rifled through the contents. There were a few T-shirts, a couple of skirts and a dress in various shades of the rainbow, plus an old pair of cut-off denim shorts. She'd make do for a few days. She turned to the wardrobe to grab a clothes hanger. Tucked in the corner beside the wardrobe was a white wooden baby's bassinette and hanging on the wardrobe doors were two long dresses in pale green silk. The bridesmaids' dresses, one for her and one for Rose.

She wondered what Scarlett and Jake would do about their wedding. So much had changed in just twenty-four hours. It was more than just Ruby's expectations of herself. Yesterday Scarlett and Jake had been counting down the days to their wedding and the birth of their first child. Now they were sitting at Rose's bedside, waiting and hoping for some good news.

A wedding and a baby. Ruby knew one could be postponed but not the other. She hoped the baby didn't decide to come early. They had enough going on at present.

She threw her clothes onto a couple of hangers and headed for the shower. She showered quickly and turned her back to the bathroom mirror as she dried herself. She hated looking at her reflection in the mirror. She disliked any form of self-examination or introspection.

She knew she wasn't particularly brilliant, like Scarlett. She was smart enough but didn't love studying and she wasn't pretty like Rose. Her face was too round, her nose was too small and she felt that her features still looked babyish despite the fact that she had just turned twenty-seven. At five feet nine inches she was tallish and model thin with no boobs to speak of. Her shoulder-length strawberry-blond locks were currently died platinum blonde, but despite regularly changing the colour of her hair she was yet to find a colour that she thought suited her. Her eyes were her best feature, large and an unusual shade of green. The colour of an emu's egg. The colour of the bridesmaids' dresses.

She wasn't dark and curvaceous like Scarlett or blonde, petite and beautiful like Rose. She didn't have Scarlett's lustrous mane of raven hair or accompanying thick dark eyelashes neither did she have Rose's perfectly proportioned heart-shaped face or dimples. She and Scarlett had their mother's long, lean legs but that was where the similarities ended.

Scarlett was the clever sister, Rose was the pretty one and Ruby was never really sure which sister she was. She knew others described her as the fun one but she also knew that she'd worked hard to cultivate that image. She wanted to be seen as the fun one, the extrovert, and she knew it was because she was scared that if she stopped and stood still she would disappear. In her mind, if people thought she was fun they would gravitate towards her and then she would know she existed and she wouldn't be lonely.

Ruby returned to her room and swapped the bath towel for a fresh singlet top and a long skirt made of a multitude of patchwork squares. It had been hot outside, the dry Adelaide summer heat was making the day almost unpleasant, and it had been warm in the ICU too.

Scarlett had left a pile of books stacked beside the bed. Ruby flicked through them as she waited for Jake. At the bottom of the pile was a Jane Austen novel, which Ruby recognised as one of Rose's favourites. She stashed it in her bag, deciding she'd take it to the hospital to read to Rose. It would help to pass the time.

As she followed Jake back into the ICU she couldn't help but notice that the new guy, the motorbike accident, had been put into the cubicle next to Rose. The nurses had removed his blankets—she obviously wasn't the only one who found ICU uncomfortably warm—and she ran her eyes over him appreciatively. His torso was bare but partly covered by his right arm, which was fixed across his chest in a blue orthopaedic sling. She could see the definition of his pectoral muscles above the sling and the ridges of his lower abdominal muscles below it. His chest was smooth and hairless and wonderfully masculine. She could feel her steps slowing as she gave herself time to appreciate his sculpted chest and arms. She couldn't blame the nurses for exposing him—something so gorgeous shouldn't be covered up.

His smooth, tanned skin was unmarked by any tattoos as far as she could see, but his youth, physique and the injuries she suspected he had still suggested a motorbike accident. Her eyes drifted up over the curve of his deltoid muscle to where his hair brushed his shoulder. His hair was long and brushed back from a strong forehead. The oxygen mask over his face had been replaced with tubing, exposing a square jaw and full lips. He reminded her of a fair-haired Greek god—dark blond and tanned and perfectly formed—but surely he had to be mortal. He'd been injured after all.

Too late she realised he was awake.

CHAPTER TWO

HE WAS AWAKE and he was watching her.

His eyes were bright blue and she could see him follow her path as she continued slowly past. Knowing she was in his sights made her blush but she managed to smile at him. There was nothing else to do. She'd been sprung admiring him. She knew it and so did he.

He grinned back, his smile full of mischief, and Ruby felt a warm glow suffuse her body and lift her spirits. She knew he'd only been in the ICU for an hour or two but already he looked far too healthy and vital for this room. Which made her wonder about his smile. She had probably imagined a connection—most likely he was still delirious and drugged and would smile at anyone.

She kept walking. Each bed was separated by a thin partition wall and at the foot of each bed was a curtain that could be pulled across for privacy. The cubicles were arranged around the outside of the room with a raised central station for the medical team. Ruby stepped into Rose's cubicle and her neighbour disappeared from view.

It felt like it had taken her several minutes to cross the room when in reality it had probably been seconds, but even though he was now out of sight his image was burnt on her retina—bright blue eyes, a tanned and ripped torso and a roguish smile. She knew the memory of his smile would get her through the rest of the day.

'How did the lumbar puncture go?' Jake asked, as he greeted Scarlett with a kiss.

'Fine, apparently. We're just waiting for the results.'

Ruby sighed. More waiting. Being impatient wasn't going to speed up the process but she didn't care, she wanted answers.

She offered to sit with Rose. She would read to her to pass the time while the others stretched their legs. As they left Ruby saw the swish of the curtain in the next cubicle as the nurse pulled it closed. Voices carried to her from the other side of the partition as she pulled the novel from her handbag.

'Is your pain relief working?' the nurse asked. 'You can top it up if you need to by pushing this button.'

'I can handle the pain,' he replied. 'What's the damage?'

His voice was deep and sent an unusual tremble through her chest. It reminded her of distant thunder as it rumbled through her. His voice matched his rugged, muscular and masculine physique perfectly.

'I need to know what injuries I sustained.'

'You have a broken collarbone, a fractured elbow and a couple of busted ribs.'

'No serious chest injuries?'

'No, but the list does go on. You also have a fractured femur.'

'Dammit.'

Ruby almost burst out laughing. She wasn't even pretending to read as she smiled to herself and continued to eavesdrop on the conversation.

'What have they done with that?' he asked.

'It's been screwed and plated.'

'How long will I be in ICU?'

'You've only just got here. What's your hurry?'

Ruby caught herself frowning as she listened to the nurse's flirty tones.

'It will give me an idea how severe my injuries are.'

'I take it you're no stranger to hospitals?'

'I've been patched up a few times.'

Ruby would swear she could hear the smile in his voice and she could imagine his bright blue eyes sparkling with just a hint of recklessness.

'You lost a lot of blood and you've just undergone major surgery. Protocol dictates that we need to keep a close eye on you for the next twenty-four hours.'

'Whose protocol?' he challenged.

'The hospital's insurance company and your team's.'

'I thought as much.'

'ICU is not such a bad place to recuperate for a few days. It's much more secure than any of the other beds, including the private rooms on the general wards. I'm guessing there may be quite a bit of interest in your story and at least we can keep journalists at bay while you're with us.'

Ruby's curiosity was piqued. She had always been a sucker for anything with a hint of difference, be it a job, a situation or, more often than not, a man. She listened with interest, waiting for further details but was left disappointed.

'Fair enough. I won't make a fuss for a day or two but I'm not a great one for standing still.'

'I think you've managed to solve that problem for a while at least. You won't be going too far at all on that broken leg.'

It went quiet in the cubicle next door and Ruby saw the nurse move on to the patient on the other side. She opened the novel and started to read but she could hear her words weren't flowing. Her mind was distracted, fixated on the motorbike man. Who was he? And why would the media be interested in him?

She forced herself to keep reading. She couldn't worry about a stranger in the bed next door. She tried choosing some of her favourite scenes, ones that showed the heroine's sense of humour, but she found herself constantly looking at Rose, waiting for a response from her, expecting to see a smile or a hint of laughter but, of course, there was nothing. Unrealistically, she'd been hoping for a miracle, hoping the story would trigger a response, and it was difficult to continue without even a flicker of encouragement from Rose.

Ruby closed the book.

'Hello? Are you still there?'

Ruby frowned. She recognised the voice. Deep and quiet, it was the motorbike man. 'Are you talking to me?' she asked.

'Yes. Do you think you could keep reading?'

Her frown deepened. 'You want to listen to a romance novel written in the nineteenth century?'

'Romance? I thought it was a comedy.'

His comment made her smile. She'd always enjoyed the unexpected humour in this book too.

'But it's not the content...I like the sound of your voice,' he said simply. 'I could listen to you read the phone book.'

Ruby laughed and opened the book again. If the motorbike man could make her laugh when she really didn't feel like it, she figured he deserved a favour. 'If it's all the same, I'll stick with Jane Austen,' she said.

She picked up from where she'd stopped but this time the words flowed far more smoothly. She lost track of time as she turned the pages, only stopping when the nurse interrupted to do Rose's obs.

Ruby took a moment to stretch her legs. At least, that was what she told herself she was doing when she stood and wandered into the cubicle next door. She wanted to know why the motorbike man was in the ICU and she was going to ask him. He'd been very quiet while she'd been reading—she'd half expected some interruptions but she'd heard nothing from him—but now she saw why.

He was asleep.

Her eyes swept over his face. His cheekbones were wide and his nose was perfectly straight and narrow, flaring ever so slightly where it ended just above full lips. His eyebrows and lashes were a shade darker than his hair and she could see the beginnings of a darker beard on his jaw. A couple of little scars marked his face, one below his eye, another on his lip, but they did nothing to detract from his looks. His dark blond hair framed his face but one stray strand lay across his cheek. Ruby was tempted to reach out and brush it away but she was afraid of waking him. He looked like he was sleeping comfortably and she didn't want to disturb him.

He had a face she suspected she could look at for hours but she could hear the nurse's footsteps moving around Rose's bed. Ruby ducked out of the cubicle before she was caught being somewhere she had no business to be.

Monday, 15th December

Sitting by Rose's bed wasn't achieving anything. Ruby had spent the whole day in ICU and nothing had changed for the better.

The doctors had confirmed that Rose had pneumococcal meningitis but if anyone expected a diagnosis to make a difference they were disappointed. Rose's condition hadn't improved and the doctors were now worried about her declining kidney function as a result of the blood poisoning. Her condition and treatment remained the same and the family just sat and waited for a sign, for anything, to indicate that she was recovering.

Ruby had chatted to Scarlett, Jake and her mother when they'd all been at Rose's bedside and when she and Rose had been alone she'd read to her and kept one ear peeled for the sound of the voice of the motorbike man next door, the man with the devilish grin and the voice like distant thunder, but it seemed he wasn't in a talkative mood today.

There was a lot more activity in the ICU and Ruby knew that there wasn't a moment when they were alone but she was disappointed he hadn't even tried to strike up a conversation with her. By the end of the day she had learned nothing further about him. She still didn't know who he was and he'd had no visitors, not a single one. He'd had no one to talk to other than the doctors and nurses and Ruby hadn't learnt anything interesting from them.

Where was his family? Where were the people who cared about him?

She supposed she could have asked him, should have asked him, but whenever she had gone in or out of Rose's

cubicle there had been one of the medical staff with him
and she hadn't been able to do more than smile at him.

She should have tried harder. She should have worked
on her timing but she was nervous, which was something quite out of character for her. Holding back was
not in her nature. Normally, if she wanted something,
whether it was information or an introduction, she would
make it happen. But the butterflies that took flight in her
stomach whenever they made eye contact were enough
to make her hesitate.

If they'd been in a social setting she would have
walked straight up to him so perhaps it was the fact
that he was at a disadvantage physically that made her
hesitant. He didn't know that she'd stood at his bedside
the night before and watched him sleep. She thought that
might freak him out so she was keeping her distance. He
had no way of getting away from her if she encroached
on his personal space. He wouldn't be able to avoid her
and she hated to think that she wouldn't know if he was
pleased with her attention or not. She didn't want him
to feel obligated to be nice to her just because he was
confined to a bed.

She didn't consider that he could easily be blunt and
tell her to leave him alone—something about the way
he smiled at her made her think he wouldn't be rude,
but she didn't want to put him in an awkward position.
So she said nothing.

By late afternoon she was tired of staring at the same
four walls. Tired of pretending everything would be fine.
Rose had made it through another twenty-four hours but
that was all that had happened. She supposed that was
better than the alternative but she had reached her limit

of being cooped up. She knew she wasn't doing a very good job of being supportive but she couldn't stay inside the hospital for a minute longer.

Lucy was coming to take over the bedside vigil from her so Ruby arranged to meet her friend Candice for dinner. The last time she'd been back to Adelaide several months earlier had been for Candice's wedding. It was strange to think that had been when Jake had been persistently pursuing Scarlett and she'd been trying to fend off his advances but not doing so very successfully. Now, months later, it was hard to imagine them not together.

Ruby and Candice had nursed together in Melbourne but had both grown up in Adelaide. In typical Adelaide fashion there were only ever three degrees of separation. Ruby and Candice had worked together, now Candice worked as a theatre nurse for emergency surgery in this hospital, where Scarlett was an anaesthetist and Jake was about to be an intern, and Candice and Jake had grown up together as family friends. If anyone understood what Ruby and her family were going through at the moment, it was Candice.

As they selected their dishes from the Thai menu Ruby filled her friend in on Rose's status before Candice moved the conversation on to 'other business', as she called it.

'So, are you bringing a plus one to Scarlett's wedding?'

Ruby shook her head.

'Why not? I know you have one, you always have one. I used to wonder how you found so many.'

'You don't wonder any more?'

'Not now that I'm married.' Candice laughed. 'It doesn't bother me any longer that you seem to have more than your fair share of men. Now that I've taken myself out of the marketplace you can have as many as you want, but I do like to meet one of them every now and again. Who's the latest?'

Ruby paused. She didn't think there was actually that much to say but it would be nice to talk about the things they always used to discuss. It would be nice to get her mind off Rose's medical predicament for just a while.

'I'm not sure that there is a latest,' she admitted.

'You're between boyfriends?'

'I'm not sure exactly.'

'How can you not be sure? What's going on?'

'Mitch was asleep when Scarlett rang me about Rose in the middle of the night. The phone call didn't wake him. I left him a note.' Mitch was a musician, a drummer, and his band had been playing at one of the local pubs that night. He'd got home late and hadn't been asleep long when Scarlett's phone call had woken Ruby. But Mitch had slept through all of that and Ruby hadn't thought it necessary to wake him. It wasn't any of his business. She hadn't thought about Mitch since she'd walked out.

'You left him a note?' Candice's tone let Ruby know exactly what she thought about that. 'Have you spoken to him?'

Ruby shook her head. 'He hasn't called me either,' she said defensively. 'We don't, didn't, have that sort of relationship.' They hadn't been like Scarlett and Jake. Or Candice and her husband, Ewan. They had both found the person they wanted to spend the rest of their life with. They had found the person who came first. Ruby had no idea what that was like.

'Well, if neither of you are prepared to pick up the

phone, you're probably perfectly matched,' Candice decided, 'but it's kind of ironic 'cos now you'll never know.'

'It doesn't matter,' Ruby said with a shrug. 'I'd never
planned to bring him home to meet my family and certainly not for Scarlett's wedding. We wouldn't have
lasted much longer anyway. I'd been seeing him for almost two months.'

Two months was her self-imposed time limit on relationships. Any longer than that and there was the chance
that one of them could start to think the relationship was
serious and that was something Ruby had always taken
pains to avoid. A serious relationship meant sharing bits
of your soul with another person. Letting them see deep
inside you. It meant taking things a step further than
sharing a bed and your body. Sharing your mind was a
far scarier proposition and not one that Ruby was particularly keen on.

In her experience people started to expect more from
a relationship as it started to edge towards three months.
Boyfriends wanted to know more about her. They would
expect to be invited to an event as her plus one. Three
months meant it was serious. It meant it would hurt if
she was abandoned.

'Besides,' she added, 'worrying about a plus one to
the wedding is irrelevant as I assume Scarlett and Jake
will postpone it. I can't imagine Scarlett will want to get
married while Rose is in hospital. She'll want to wait
until Rose has recovered.' Ruby couldn't voice the alternative. That Rose might not get better.

'They haven't said what they're planning on doing?'

Ruby shook her head. 'No. It seems kind of an odd
conversation to have in the ICU. We tend to talk about
what the doctor's latest update means and what treat-

ment Rose should have. I think everyone is just avoiding the topic of anything to do with the future. I don't
think any of us can think more than a day ahead at this
stage. So it means we sit there not really talking about
much at all. It's no wonder the days seem interminably
long in Intensive Care, but it's all we can do. Just be
there for Rose.'

'Let's hope she's out of there soon and then a few
more of us can split the shifts and visit her.'

Access to the ICU was restricted to family members
only, and that reminded Ruby of the lonely motorbike
man. She wondered why she hadn't thought to ask Candice for information. She might have even been working on the day he had been brought in. She might be
the one person Ruby knew who would have the low-
down on him.

'Speaking of visiting, there's a guy in the bed next to
Rose who hasn't had any visitors at all. He was brought
into ICU yesterday. He looked as though he would have
come through Emergency first. Were you working? Do
you know anything about him?'

Candice grinned. 'I wasn't working but I heard about
him. He's into motorsport apparently, a racing-car driver
or something. By all reports, he'd done a fair bit of damage to himself but the girls were still very complimen-
tary about him.' Her grin widened. 'It's not every day
they get to see quite such a glorious naked man. Even
if they did have to cover him with sterile drapes, they
copped quite an eyeful in between times.'

Ruby's imagination quickly added what Candice was
describing to what she'd already seen for herself and
created a rather glorious picture. Almost real enough
to make her blush. 'Do you know his name?' she asked.

'Neil? No, that's not right.' Candice shook her head. 'Noel maybe? Something starting with an N anyway. The girls weren't interested in his name.' She laughed. 'But I can find out if you like.'

'No, that's okay. I was just curious.' She should have checked his chart while he slept, just to find out his name, but that seemed like invading his privacy just a little too much.

'That would make you just one in a long line, from what I hear.'

Ruby was curious but she'd hoped Candice would have been able to give her a name or something to enable her to do some research when she got home. She didn't want to think of it as cyber-stalking but wasn't that one of the purposes of the internet? But she still didn't have enough to go on.

It was ridiculous. She was never going to find out anything about him. She rather liked the fantasy of the lonely bachelor that she'd built up around him but she knew it was probably a complete fallacy. She knew the simplest way to get some answers would be to strike up a conversation with him. If she wanted to know more, she was going to have to drum up some courage and ask him herself.

Normally she was up for a bit of fun, some harmless flirtation, as much as the next person. All right, usually a bit more than the next person. A girl had to know how to have fun but even she wasn't sure that an intensive care unit was the appropriate place to attempt to pick up a man. She was sure it wouldn't make the list in a women's magazine when they printed their articles on the top ten places to meet men. Not unless you worked there and then it could technically come under the heading of a workplace.

And although Ruby couldn't be accused of being mainstream in her approach to dating, or even meeting men, even she wasn't convinced that having an eye on a man who was lying in an ICU, no matter how hot he looked, was acceptable in the dating jungle.

Tuesday, 16th December

But nothing ventured, nothing gained was her motto, and the next morning was as good a time as any to venture, she decided as she keyed in the code to open the door into the ICU. Now that she knew he wasn't an axe murderer or serial killer, she could relax. Her judgement had been known to let her down on occasion.

She summoned up her courage and pushed the door open. She'd check on Rose and then strike up a conversation. There'd be no harm in saying a simple 'Hello' as she walked past. She didn't need to crowd him. She could say hello and then the ball would be in his court. If he wanted to engage her in conversation she'd be a willing participant. He'd had no visitors, perhaps she could offer to help. There must be something he needed and, if not, at least she would have broken the ice.

She was all ready to flash him her best smile as she made her way to Rose's cubicle but his bed was empty, stripped of its sheets, leaving the mattress exposed, the machines all neatly packed away. The bed looked as though it had never been occupied.

The adrenalin that had been coursing through her body clumped together to form a little ball of lead in her chest and plummeted to the pit of her stomach, leaving her feeling flat.

He was gone and she'd missed her chance.

She couldn't believe it.

It wasn't really in her nature to be hesitant and she couldn't explain why she'd held back. But she had and now she would never know anything more about him. Disappointment flooded her, joining the ball of lead in her gut.

She stepped past the empty bed and into Rose's cubicle. Seeing Rose still lying inert, her condition obviously unchanged, and hearing the mechanical suck and hiss of the ventilator didn't do anything to lift her spirits.

She leant over and squeezed Rose's hand in greeting before kissing her cheek. Even if Rose wasn't responding she had to let her sister know she was there. She kissed her mother next and then sank into a chair beside Lucy.

'Has there been any change?' she asked.

Lucy shook her head. 'No, but we've passed the forty-eight-hour mark.'

Ruby knew that was a big milestone but what she didn't know was how much that meant if Rose still hadn't shown any signs of improvement.

'Have the doctors seen her this morning?'

'Yes, and they seem to think it's a positive that Rose hasn't declined any further.' Ruby could hear the hopeful note in her mum's voice, as if praying for Rose's recovery would be enough to make it happen. That might have worked if they'd been a religious family but they weren't. But, still, none of them were prepared to discuss anything other than the idea that Rose would recover, even though they all knew there were no guarantees. They only had their belief to get them through this. 'Will you be able to stay until she's better?' Lucy added.

Ruby nodded. She wouldn't leave while Rose was critically ill. She'd stay as long as she could and hopefully that would be long enough.

'What about work? Can you get extra time off?'

Ruby hadn't thought about work since she'd jumped on a plane before sunrise on Sunday and her mother's question made her realise she hadn't actually told work she was away. She'd been working as an agency nurse in Byron Bay. She'd been working as an agency nurse for years actually as the flexibility suited her. There was no commitment. She could almost come and go as she pleased, which she did on a fairly frequent basis. When she'd decided she'd had enough of one place she could up and leave without feeling like she was leaving an employer in the lurch.

Had she missed a shift? She couldn't remember. She certainly hadn't had a phone call telling her she'd forgotten to turn up. She did a quick calculation. Today was Monday, wasn't it? No, Tuesday. That was okay, her next shift wasn't until tomorrow. She had time to sort that out.

'Time off isn't a problem,' she told Lucy. 'I'll just tell the agency I'm unavailable.'

Getting days off wasn't difficult but losing the pay cheque would hurt. But there wasn't anything she could do about that. She wasn't leaving until Rose was out of the woods.

'Are you still working agency? You don't want something more permanent?'

Lucy had been working for the same aged care facility for ever. Ruby knew she was very attached to the residents but they didn't live forever. In normal nursing

patients came and went and Ruby couldn't see what difference having a permanent job would make to her life
when there was so much change anyway. Ruby didn't
want to form attachments, it would make leaving difficult.

'It's just as well I'm doing agency work as it meant I
could jump on a plane and come to Adelaide without letting anyone down,' she said, but she knew better than to
expect that to be the end of the conversation. She waited
for the inevitable question.

'You don't want to settle down?'

There it was. Their conversations always seemed to
come back to that. No matter what they were discuss-
ing, her mother always seemed to be able to raise the
topic of settling down.

By the age of twenty-six Lucy had been a mother of
three but Ruby knew it hadn't all been by choice and
she had no intention of making the same mistakes her
mother had made. She chose to ignore the fact that not
only had she made some of the same mistakes, she had
also made other, different, ones and now she was trying just to get through life. She wanted company but she
didn't want commitment. She didn't want to share her
private thoughts or her history with anyone else.

She could feel her hackles rising.

She knew she should be mature enough not to fight
with her mother, especially not at the moment next to
her sister's ICU bed. Rose always tried to avoid con-
frontation and Ruby didn't want to get into a fight here
in case Rose could hear them. She knew she wouldn't
have given work a second thought if Lucy hadn't asked
about it and that realisation put a match to her already

short fuse. She needed to remove herself from the situation before Lucy could ask any more questions.

'Have you eaten today?' she asked. She needed some breathing space and a quick trip to the hospital kiosk would give her a chance to get it. 'I'm starving. I skipped breakfast so I might go and grab something to eat. Would you like something?' She couldn't remember when she'd last seen her mother eat and, as she expected, Lucy declined her offer.

As she left the ICU she couldn't help but look at the empty space in the cubicle beside Rose. She hoped the vacant bed meant he'd been moved because he was recovering well. She didn't want to think that things might have gone from bad to worse.

She kept her eyes peeled for him as she made her way along the hospital corridors but he was nowhere to be seen. It wasn't as though she'd really expected to bump into him but she still felt a frisson of disappointment as she stepped up to the counter of the hospital kiosk and placed her order.

She just wanted to see him once more. She needed to know he was okay.

She picked up her green tea and vegetarian wrap and turned from the counter and found the person she'd been searching for. He was sitting on the opposite side of the room, watching her with his bright blue eyes.

It had been twenty-four hours since she'd seen him and she couldn't help but think what a difference a day made. One day ago he'd been in an intensive care bed and now he was dressed and sitting in the hospital kiosk. Watching her.

Although he was on the far side of a crowded room Ruby would have sworn they had the place to themselves. She certainly wasn't aware of anyone else. Not while he was watching her. Even from a distance the colour of his eyes was a vivid blue and somehow he had become familiar to her despite the fact she still had no idea who he was.

He smiled and her heart skipped a beat.

He didn't look surprised to see her. Neither did he seem embarrassed to be caught watching her. If she didn't know better she would think he'd been waiting for her.

Her heart pounded in her chest as she walked towards him. She told herself she had to walk past him to get out of the kiosk but there were actually several different exits, she could have easily chosen a different route, but her feet were already moving in his direction. It was no use pretending she didn't want to see him; for the past two days she'd thought of nothing else except her sister and the stranger in the bed next to her.

She was three steps away when she discovered that the path she'd taken was blocked by his wheelchair. She hesitated and looked up, meeting his eyes, before continuing on another step.

'Hello.' His voice rumbled through her. It was deep and strong but quiet. It sounded as though he was far away but it was loud enough to bring her to a stop beside him. It was only one little word, two syllables, but to Ruby's ears it was so much more than a simple greeting. To Ruby it was the start of something more.

CHAPTER THREE

'HELLO,' SHE MANAGED in reply, before her words disappeared and she stood in front of him completely speechless. She wasn't normally tongue-tied and she knew she'd had a whole conversation planned for when she next saw him but that had been based on the expectation that he would still be in the ICU. Not sitting in the middle of a busy kiosk looking a picture of health.

Someone had washed his hair and Ruby could see now that it was more blond than brown. It swept back from his forehead in a widow's peak, exposing his strong brow and allowing his blue eyes to shine, and hung to his jaw line, framing and accentuating the oval shape of his face. Despite the length of his hair and the fullness of his lips his was a masculine face, and as if to reinforce the fact his jaw was darkened by the growth of a new beard. In contrast to his hair his three-day designer stubble was more brown than blond. His face was pleasant and friendly and his smile was brilliant.

Ruby's eyes dropped from his lips to his body. His right arm was tucked inside his T-shirt and she could see the tell-tale bumps and lumps from the sling, but his left arm was tanned and muscly, really muscly, and lightly dusted with fair hair.

He was wearing shorts and a hinged knee brace was fitted over his right leg. She remembered the list of injuries the nurse had rattled off. A fractured clavicle, ribs, elbow and femur. He'd certainly done a good job on himself. From the neck down he didn't really look in a fit state to be out of the ward, let alone left abandoned in the kiosk.

'Would you do me a favour?' he asked, as Ruby finished her inspection and lifted her eyes back up to his face. She blushed slightly. She'd been caught blatantly checking him out.

Anything, she thought, but she just nodded in reply, still unable to find her voice.

At least he seemed willing and able to carry on a conversation. 'Would you mind pushing me outside? I'd really love to get into the sunshine but I can't move this damn thing without help,' he said, as he used his head to gesture towards his chest and his arm where it lay trapped in the sling. 'Actually, that's not quite true,' he clarified. 'I can move but only if I'm happy to go round in circles.'

He smiled at her and Ruby's heart skipped another beat. His smile was full of cheek and made his blue eyes sparkle. She could feel herself being taken in by his charm. He was handsome and charismatic and in her experience that was a dangerous combination. And she'd always been a sucker for danger.

She tilted her head to one side as she studied him. 'How did you get down here?' she asked. Her voice was husky. That wasn't unusual but even to her ears it sounded huskier than normal, as if it had been days, not minutes, since she'd used it.

'I bribed a nurse,' he said with a wink.

Ruby felt the heat from his gaze course through her and she could just imagine the nurses falling over themselves to help him. She knew they'd normally be too busy to lend a hand—if a patient wanted to get outside they'd have to do so under their own steam—but seeing his smile and his automatic wink she knew just how that scene would have played out.

She raised one eyebrow. 'I bet it was a young nurse.'

He laughed, or rather he began to laugh before he stopped short and winced, and Ruby realised his broken ribs must have been protesting, but even so the brief sound of his laugh reverberated through her and made her smile along with him.

'It was,' he admitted. 'So, will you help me? I've had enough of being cooped up inside.'

She couldn't blame the nurse who'd fallen for his charms, she could see he'd be difficult to resist and she could well imagine how restless he was feeling. Despite the fact he was wheelchair-bound with a rather cumbersome-looking brace on his leg, he still looked too vital, too energetic to tolerate being stuck inside.

'Sure, but you'll have to hold this for me,' she said, as she handed him her lunch.

He took her food, balancing it in his lap along with his own cup and stabilising it all with his left hand and forearm.

Ruby bent down to release the wheelchair brakes, a co-conspirator to his escape. She could smell the coffee in his cup as she flicked off the right brake. As she leaned behind him and flicked off the left one her hair brushed over his shoulder—she was close enough now to smell him too. His hair smelt faintly of limes. He smelt fresh and far better than he should considering he'd spent the past couple of days in a hospital bed. Ruby knew from looking at his leg that he wouldn't have been able to shower himself and she wondered which nurse had volunteered to wash his hair and give him a sponge bath.

She felt her temperature rise as the thought of sponging him down took hold. She ran her eyes over the muscles in his left leg as her mind wandered. She forced herself to straighten up before she was tempted to reach out and run a hand down his thigh, only to find herself, once again, under the scrutiny of his blue-eyed gaze. She wondered if he could guess what she was thinking. She hoped not.

She stood behind him and gripped the handles of the wheelchair, glad of a reason to break eye contact. She gathered her errant thoughts together and pushed him out through the kiosk doors.

Outside several picnic tables and benches were scattered around a paved courtyard and shaded by a couple of large elm trees. It was late in the morning, well before a regular lunchtime, and the courtyard was virtually deserted. Ruby pushed the wheelchair towards a picnic bench.

'Where would you like me to put you?' she asked.

'Here's fine.' His back was towards the morning sun and Ruby could see the soft golden hairs on his forearm as the sunlight kissed his skin. 'Will you keep me company?' he asked, as she flicked the brakes on his wheelchair, locking him in position.

She hesitated. The old Ruby wouldn't have hesitated but she was making a conscious effort not to always put herself first but to consider other people's needs. Her family's, for instance. Would anyone miss her? Should she be at Rose's bedside?

'You'd be doing me a favour,' he added, as he waited for her reply. 'I'm tired of my own company. You could save me from sitting here and talking to myself.'

Rose had company, Ruby told herself. Lucy was with her and surely they could spare her while she ate her brunch.

'That doesn't sound very enticing, does it? It makes me sound boring. I'll admit to being bored but I hope I'm not boring,' he added, when she still didn't answer.

By way of an answer, Ruby sat on the bench in the shade of one of the elm trees. Her fair skin burnt easily and even though it wasn't yet midday she knew better than to expose herself to the summer sun. He smiled at her as she sat down and Ruby knew she'd made a good decision.

'I'm Noah,' he told her, as he handed her tea over.

Noah.

Not Noel. Not Neil. Noah. She liked Noah far better. His name suited him. He looked strong and capable. He looked like a man who would take charge. He looked like a man who could handle himself physically. A man who worked with his hands.

If he was into racing cars, as Candice had proposed, then she guessed he did all those things, just not in the way she'd first imagined. He would need physical strength in his job. Mental strength as well.

He was passing her the wrap. 'Do you have a name?'

Her fingers brushed his as she took the wrap and it took her a second or two to answer as her brain was busy trying to process his question and deal with the sensations running through her.

'Ruby.'

'That's a pretty name.'

'Do you say that to all the girls?'

'Only when it's true.'

He was watching her with his bright blue eyes and his attention sent a shiver of expectation through her that made her hands shake as she undid her wrap.

'You've coloured your hair,' he said, as he sipped his coffee.

Ruby self-consciously put a hand to her head.

'Your hair wasn't pink yesterday, was it?' he asked.

She shook her head. Her natural strawberry blond locks had been dyed platinum blond until earlier today when she'd updated her colour. Her hair was now pale pink and she was pleased with the result. 'I coloured it this morning.'

'Good. I recognised your voice but the colour of your hair confused me. I was worried my concussion had ruined either my eyesight or my memory or that the drugs they're giving me are way stronger than I need them to be.'

Ruby smiled. 'I did this for Rose.'

'She's your sister? In ICU?'

She nodded. 'I'm constantly changing the colour of my hair and when Rose and I speak on the phone she always wants to know what colour it is. Pink is her favourite. I thought maybe it would be enough to elicit a response.'

'And?'

Ruby shook her head. 'Nothing.'

She wasn't sure why she told Noah all that. She usually avoided talking about anything personal and she didn't want to talk about Rose. She'd rather talk about him.

'I heard you were in a car accident,' she said, swing-

ing the conversation back to him. Talking about him
seemed safer. It was far less emotional and there was
less of a chance of her making an idiot of herself by
bursting into tears.

'Who told you that?'

She smiled. 'I have friends in high places.'

He looked a little panicked and Ruby suddenly remembered the nurse talking about the media. She took
pity on him. 'I'm a nurse, we talk.'

'You work here?'

'No. But I have friends who do. But don't worry, that's
all I know. I didn't know your name until you told me.
So, are you going to tell me what happened? I was sure
you'd crashed a motorbike, not a car.'

'A motorbike? Why?'

Because she could picture him astride a motorbike.
She could almost hear the deep throaty growl of the engine as it throbbed between his powerful thighs. She
could see him push his hair back from his forehead as
he removed his helmet. She could picture him placing
it between his thighs and leaning forwards onto it as he
invited her to go for a ride. She had several fantasies involving men on motorbikes and he fitted them perfectly
but she couldn't tell him any of that.

She kept it simple. 'You look like a motorbike type
of guy. Except for the lack of tattoos.'

He grinned and raised an eyebrow. 'You were looking for tattoos?'

She blushed and he chuckled.

'Motorbikes are far too dangerous,' he added.

'Says a man who races cars for a living.'

'I thought you didn't know anything about me?'

'I promise, that's it. What else should I know? Are

you famous? The nurse was taking about the media not having access to the ICU. Should I recognise you?'

'You mean you don't?'

His voice was teasing. It was deep and throaty and she couldn't decide if it was more like the motorbike engine in her imagination or distant thunder, but the sound was soothing and she felt herself relax for the first time since she'd landed in Adelaide. She'd been wound up like a spring and she could feel herself unwinding as she sat in the company of this divine hunk of a man.

'Only from the ICU,' she told him.

'You don't read motoring magazines?'

'Not if I can help it.'

'That's right,' he said, 'romance novels are your thing. I'm sorry I didn't thank you for reading to me. I wasn't in a very sociable mood yesterday. I hate being out of action but I enjoyed listening to you, you have a very sexy voice.'

His comment flustered her. He was very direct. She was almost as uncomfortable with receiving a compliment as she was talking about herself so she changed the subject again.

'It was my pleasure but now you need to answer my question. Are you famous? Do we need to be worried about the paparazzi with long lenses?'

'No. My team put out a press release. The media have their story and it wasn't nearly as exciting as they would have liked.'

'Your team?'

'I drive V8 race cars. That's my job but I'm just part of a team. I crashed a car but it was only in testing.'

'Only?'

He nodded. 'It's far better to crash during testing than

in a race. The team has more time to repair things but they still weren't very happy with me. I turned months of work into a mass of crumpled metal. Luckily, it turns out it wasn't my fault. It was a mechanical failure so now I'm back in their good books.'

'You think you're lucky it wasn't your fault. How about lucky you're still alive!'

He shrugged. 'It was no big deal. The media have their story. It was an engineering problem with the car, not driver error. It didn't happen during an event and I don't have any life-threatening injuries. It's not exciting enough for front-page news.'

It sounded exciting enough to Ruby.

'If it happened in a couple of months' time they'd be more interested,' he added.

'What happens in a couple of months?'

'The racing season would be about to start. The media will be looking for stories then.'

Ruby frowned. 'You're not planning on being ready to race in a few weeks, are you?'

'I'm going to give it my best shot. I have almost twelve weeks. I think I'm in with a chance.'

'Really? You have a busted arm, collarbone, leg and ribs and you think you'll be racing cars again in a few weeks?' From what Ruby could remember from her stints in orthopaedics, he'd be cutting it fine.

'Don't forget the concussion,' he said. 'But my leg has been pinned, my elbow is only cracked and my collarbone and ribs will heal in no time.'

Ruby raised her eyebrows but tried to keep quiet. It wasn't her place to make a judgement. Stranger things had happened and many times she'd seen how a positive mental attitude could overcome the most difficult physical problems. But even so...

'Even if you are healed, you'd have to be crazy to put yourself back in a car. The safety features must leave a lot to be desired if you've sustained these sorts of injuries.' She thought perhaps he was a little bit crazy but that wasn't all that surprising. You'd have to be a little bit mad to make your living from racing cars.

'It was the safety features that *gave* me some of these injuries. The harness broke a couple of my ribs and my helmet cracked my collarbone. But I've had worse.'

Definitely a little bit crazy, she decided.

'It's a challenge but I like a challenge.'

He was watching her closely as he said this and Ruby could see the challenge in his eyes. He was just her type—sexy, a little bit dangerous and a risk-taker. She was always attracted to men who were a little bit different. It kept life interesting.

He was rubbing his temple with his left hand, his biceps muscle flexing as he moved his hand to the other side of his head.

'Are you okay?' she asked.

'Bit of a headache.'

Great attention to detail, Rubes. Terrific nursing skills. He'd told her he had concussion and he was probably due some pain relief too.

'You probably shouldn't have been sitting in the sun,' she said. She stood up and collected their rubbish and threw it into the bin. 'Come on, I'll take you back inside.' It was time she got back to Rose anyway. She couldn't hide out here for ever, as tempting as that was. She needed to do her bit.

She stopped at a vending machine in the hospital entrance and bought a bottle of water.

'Here, I think you should rehydrate yourself,' she said as she handed him the bottle. He drank it as he directed her to one of the side rooms on the orthopaedic ward.

'Let me give you some money for the water,' he said as she wheeled him into his private room. He must have good health insurance but, then, she guessed he'd need it in his line of work.

'Don't worry about it. You can owe me.'

'As long as you make sure you come back to collect.'

'Oh, I will,' she said.

She was going to make sure she saw him again.

He could be a good distraction for her while Rose was in hospital. She could have a bit of company and a bit of fun. She didn't want to be a third wheel in Scarlett's relationship or in Candice's and she couldn't spend every minute with her mum. No matter how supportive she wanted to be, she knew that would end in tears and neither of them needed that stress.

In just a very short space of time Noah had cheered her up. There had been no awkwardness between them. Ruby had felt as though they were continuing a conversation they'd started before. It didn't feel as though she was making a new acquaintance but rather catching up with an old friend. It was weird but nice. Comforting. She had no idea if he'd felt the same but she figured she'd find out.

She returned to ICU feeling far more positive about the world. Seeing him had been a bright spot in her day.

The only bright spot.

And now that she knew where to find him she was determined to see him again.

Wednesday, 17th December

Noah had sweated through his morning exercise session with the physiotherapist. He always gave everything one hundred and ten per cent and his rehabilitation would be no exception. He knew he needed to be vigilant about his exercise programme if he had any hope of getting back behind the wheel of his race car in time for the opening event of the season, but he had additional motivation today. He'd pushed himself hard, hoping that exercise would provide a distraction from his constant thoughts about a slip of a girl with amazing legs and pink hair.

The physiotherapist had remonstrated with him a couple of times when he'd lost focus, when his mind had drifted off as he'd recalled the husky sound of her voice, the smattering of freckles that dusted her upturned nose and the smoothness of her thighs below the frayed hems of her tiny denim shorts. He liked her legs almost as much as he liked her voice.

But it had been her voice that had initially snookered him and he'd been thinking of her ever since he'd first heard her husky, throaty tones. He had been furious about the accident and irritated to find himself in ICU, but he'd resigned himself to the fact that he was stuck there for at least twenty-four hours when she had begun to read in her sexy, deep voice and he'd forgotten to be annoyed. He hadn't really paid much attention to the story but her voice had soothed him and excited him at the same time.

She had fascinated him from the moment she had started talking. She would make a good jazz singer. Her voice was smoky and sultry and listening to her had made ICU tolerable, and as much as he'd wanted to get out of there part of him had been sorry to go. He should have spoken to her when he'd had the chance but he'd been in too much pain. And that had been a mistake. Once he was transferred there was no guarantee he'd ever see her again.

And that was when he'd decided to work hard on his exercises and use his medication to control the pain. He would be a model patient. He knew the benefits that could bring, and he was certain that if he combined that with his infamous charm he should be able to persuade at least some of the nurses to help him out in his quest to track her down. Not that he intended to outline his exact plans to them, they didn't need to know all the details. And then, with relatively little effort, he'd found her.

She wasn't a blonde anymore but that was irrelevant. She still had the sexiest voice he'd ever heard and she'd promised to come back. Now he was just killing time while he waited.

He wasn't worried about her keeping her word. He knew when someone was interested and he was certain she was just as interested in him as he was in her. He hadn't been able to get Ruby out of his head.

He was contemplating doing a few more upper-limb exercises just to pass the time when a knock on his door distracted him. The medical staff never knocked and the cleaners had already been. He hoped it was Ruby, even though he knew it could just be the kitchen staff coming to collect his lunch tray.

The door opened and she appeared. Her hair was still pink and there was a smile in her green eyes that made it feel like the sun had just been switched on.

'Good morning,' he said. 'Have you come to collect on that drink I owe you?'

'Yep. And I wondered if you felt like playing hooky?'

He grinned. His day had just improved considerably. 'Do I need to be over eighteen?'

'Slow down, Romeo. I might not be known for my athletic ability but at the moment I can outrun you so you'll have to behave. I thought you might like to get outside.'

'Sure.'

She stepped into his room. She was wearing a tiny pair of denim shorts, the same pair she'd worn yesterday if he remembered correctly, and he knew he wouldn't have forgotten. The shorts showed off her legs and he let his gaze run over them in appreciation. They were incredible. Long and lean and toned. Her toenails were bright purple and her hair was pink. She wore a green T-shirt that matched her eyes and hung loosely on her slim frame. She was a kaleidoscope of colour and she brightened his room and his mood.

She reached out and took the bread roll from his lunch tray, which was yet to be cleared.

'Are you hungry?' he asked.

'No. It's not for me. I had something a bit more adventurous than the kiosk courtyard in mind,' she said as she dropped the roll into her bag. 'I'm kidnapping you. Just for an hour or so. Is that okay?'

That was perfectly okay as far as he was concerned.

Her small cotton bag, heavily decorated with shiny bits, was slung across her body. She pulled a pair of sunglasses from the bag and handed them to him.

'What are these for?' he asked.

'I'm being a responsible kidnapper. I need to get outside and I'm taking you with me but I don't want you to get another headache from the sun.'

He slipped the sunglasses on and looked into the mirror on the wall opposite his bed. He looked ridiculous. 'I think these might be the ugliest sunglasses I've ever seen.'

'Then you'd be wrong. They were actually the pick of the bunch in the hospital gift shop.'

He took the glasses off and stuck them on top of his head. 'You're kidding me.'

'Yep, but you'll have to suck it up, they're the best you've got.' She laughed. Her laugh was loud and contagious. She laughed like she really meant it, like she was really amused, and her laugh was infectious. She was grinning widely and he could see that her left eye tooth was a little crooked. She was adorable and he felt a hundred per cent better for her company.

'Where are you taking me?'

'Not far but I need to get away from the hospital for a bit. I need to clear my head.'

'What's happened? How are things with Rose?'

'Still the same and I can't spend all day sitting in ICU, I get too frustrated.'

'There's been no improvement?'

Ruby shook her head. 'No. And the doctors think that the longer she shows no sign of improvement the worse her prognosis is.'

'They could be wrong. I've known doctors to be wrong before.'

Ruby smiled but it wasn't the full-blown smile that lit up her face. It was a cautious half smile. 'I'm a nurse, don't forget. I've known them to be wrong before too, but I also know the odds for bacterial meningitis,' she said, as she fetched his wheelchair from the corner of the room. 'Do you mind if we don't talk about Rose? I

just want to have some fun for a while. Do you need a
hand to get into the chair?'

Noah shook his head. 'No. If you bring it closer I
can manage.'

He took his wallet from the bedside cabinet and stood
on his left leg while he stuffed the wallet into the front
pocket of his shorts. She hovered over him as he transferred himself into the wheelchair. He was a tall man,
almost six feet three inches, and Ruby's head was tucked
underneath his chin. He could smell her hair. She smelt
like a flower garden.

He swivelled around forty-five degrees and lowered
himself into the chair. Sitting down brought his eyes in
line with her thighs. Her legs looked smooth and soft
and he was tempted to reach out and stroke her skin.
But before he could move she had released his brakes
and stepped in behind him. Her floral scent wafted over
him again.

She pushed him out of his room and then parked him
at the nurses' station, giving him instructions to tell the
nurses he'd be back in an hour. While he was doing as
he was told he saw her swipe a couple more bread rolls
from the lunch trays that had been stacked into the ca-
tering trolleys and left in the corridor. These joined the
one already in her bag and he wondered what on earth
she planned to do with them.

Ruby paused out the front of the hospital and delved
into her sequined bag. She pulled out a floppy hat and
jammed it onto her head. She was starting to remind
him of Mary Poppins and he wondered what else she
had stashed in the bag. She looked fabulously quirky but
her full lips, pert nose and round face, which was at odds
with the slightness of her figure, combined together to

make her look very young. He should find out how old she was. Being a nurse, she'd have to be at least twenty-one but she could have passed for seventeen.

'Sunglasses on,' she instructed, as her wide red mouth broke into a smile. She waited for him to put the hideous glasses on before she pushed him out onto North Terrace and turned left.

Noah was familiar with these streets. The hospital was close to the V8 street-racing circuit that ran through the eastern parklands of the city and along the nearby roads. Ruby pushed him east for a hundred metres before taking him through the ornate, wrought-iron gates of the Botanic Gardens. They meandered slowly along the paths past green lawns and towering trees. Noah had spent a lot of time in the city over the past few years but had never been into the gardens. Despite the fact that they were only a few hundred metres from the city traffic, he had an immediate sense of peace and tranquillity, which was a welcome change after the continuous noise and activity of the hospital.

Ruby turned off the main path and brought him to a stop next to a large lake. The moment they stopped, several curious ducks paddled over to inspect them. He watched as Ruby took a couple of the bread rolls from her bag and proceeded to break off small pieces and throw them into the lake, creating chaos amongst the ducks. Finally, he knew why she'd swiped the rolls.

Outside, surrounded by the foliage and greenery of the gardens, she looked even more vital. She was bright against the botanical backdrop and she looked perfectly at home. She reminded him of a flamingo, with her long legs and pink hair and the water of the lake behind her.

He knew that if he turned his head and looked back

over his shoulder he would be able to see the tops of the hospital buildings poking above the trees but he didn't want to turn his head. He didn't want to look away from Ruby. He stayed still, happily content to sit and watch. It wasn't often that he got a chance to be quiet and still. While he loved his job, by definition it meant he was constantly on the go in a noisy environment. Peace and tranquillity were something he'd learnt to savour.

'This was a brilliant idea,' he told her.

'Oh, I'm full of good ideas,' she said as she turned and smiled at him and he had a sudden, overwhelming urge to pull her down to him and kiss her smiling mouth.

CHAPTER FOUR

HE WONDERED HOW she'd taste. Of strawberries, he imagined.

He wondered how she'd react.

'Here,' she said, as she put several pieces of torn-apart bread roll into his lap. 'It's your turn. Tell me,' she asked, as he attempted to throw bread to the ducks with his left hand, 'how does someone get a job as a racing-car driver?'

'I started like most kids, I guess,' he replied, as a turtle popped its head out of the lake and snagged a piece of bread before disappearing back into the murky depths. 'I grew up on a sheep station in western New South Wales and we used to ride around the farm on horses and motorbikes. That's how I know motorbikes are dangerous.

'Then I got into go-kart racing. It's quite competitive among the kids and we could race go-karts before we could get a normal driver's licence. There were plenty of regular competitions and if you're good enough, someone takes notice and eventually offers you a drive in a real car. You work your way up through the different classes until you end up at the top. Which in Australia is either in championship cars or in V8s. Dad took me to watch the V8s racing at Bathurst when I was about thirteen and I've been hooked on them ever since.'

'So it's a real job?' she asked. 'What do you write when you have to fill in a form and there's a box marked "Occupation"?'

'Yes, it's a real job.' He laughed as he threw the last of the bread into the lake. 'I write "Professional Athlete" on the form.'

'Really? You call yourself an athlete?'

She was smiling at him, not taking either of them seriously.

'You might be surprised at how physically demanding it is.'

'I might indeed.' She grinned and he watched as she looked him over. He knew he was in good physical shape. He knew how much effort he put into staying fit and he was more than happy for her to give him the once-over. He just hoped she liked what she saw.

'And is your family still in country New South Wales? Is that why you haven't had many visitors?'

She had been paying attention. He nodded. 'Dad has just had a hip replacement so he can't travel and Mum is home with him. But I doubt they would have made the trip to see me even if they could.'

'Why not?'

'Because, in the scheme of things, my injuries are relatively minor. Getting injured goes hand in hand with racing. I can't expect them to drop everything whenever I crash a car.'

'Do you do it a lot?'

'No, thank goodness. But I've been racing professionally for eight years—I've had my share of accidents.'

'So who does look after you when you're injured?'

'No one.'

'No girlfriend? No wife?'

'Not any more.' Noah removed his sunglasses. They were sitting in the shade of a willow tree and if they were going to have this conversation he wanted to be able to see her clearly. 'I'm divorced.'

'Divorced?'

When he nodded she asked, 'What was her name?

'Steph.'

'Do you mind talking about her?'

Ruby had the most incredible enormous green eyes. They reminded him of the colour of the waterholes on the farm where the oil from the leaves of the overhanging eucalyptus turned the water green, and he knew that as long as he was looking into her eyes he'd tell her anything she wanted to know.

He shook his head. 'No. It was a long time ago.'

'Where did you meet her?'

'We grew up together. Steph was the daughter of the town vet. She spent a lot of time at our place and we went to school together.'

'You were friends?'

He nodded. 'And things would have been better all round if we'd left it that way.'

'What happened?'

'We were young. Our marriage was an impulse and when the dust settled she decided that real life with me didn't suit her. She didn't like living out of a suitcase. She wanted to settle down and have a family. Now she does.'

'And you're okay with that?'

'We got married for all the wrong reasons and there weren't enough other reasons to stay together. It's not really in my nature to give up but we should never have got married in the first place. People make mistakes. You learn from them and move on. Now, yesterday I insisted I wasn't boring but I'm starting to get bored with the sound of my own voice. It's time for me to listen to you. Tell me something I should know.'

'I can't think of anything.'

'I'll make it easy for you.' He picked up her left hand. Her hand was tiny and slight in his palm. There was no ring on her ring finger. 'No husband?' She shook her head as he turned her hand over. He was reluctant to let her go. Her hand fitted so perfectly into his. 'What about a boyfriend?'

'I'm not sure.'

'What does that mean?'

'I walked out four days ago when I got the phone call about Rose. I don't think I'll be going back.'

'You haven't seen him for four days?'

'No.'

'Have you spoken to him?'

She shook her head. 'I wouldn't know what to say. We didn't have the sort of relationship where we talked much.'

'Ah.' He grinned and raised an eyebrow.

'Stop it.' She laughed and pulled her hand from his. 'That's not what I meant.'

His comment had the desired effect. He'd wanted to lighten the tension.

'So, do you think he knows it's over?' he asked.

Noah liked this girl. She stirred all the right emotions in him. Physically he was attracted to her. He loved her voice, her laugh, her legs, the way her face came to life when something amused her, and he wanted to spend time getting to know her. She was adorable—cute, funny and sexy—but he wasn't going to make a move if she was already in a relationship. That never ended well for anyone.

Ruby shrugged. 'I don't expect he'll care. And chances are, by the time I get back to Byron Bay, he would have moved on. He's a drummer in a band. If they get a gig somewhere else they'll head off.'

That sounded to him like Ruby was single. He was going to assume as much anyway.

'You live in Byron Bay?'

'For the moment.'

He was beginning to think she was well named. Getting information out of her was like drawing blood out of a stone but he was determined to find out more about her.

'You're just down the road from me,' he told her. 'I live on the Sunshine Coast when I'm not travelling around the country.'

'So what are you doing here?'

It seemed she was done talking about herself. He'd noticed before that she changed the subject whenever he asked her a personal question and the first chance she got to turn the conversation back to him she took it. He wanted to know more about her but he didn't want to frighten her off so he went with the change of topic. He hoped there'd be time later to get to know her better but he was smart enough to realise that if he scared her now he'd be ruining those chances.

'The cars are built here. My mechanics were doing modifications and organised testing at a race track north of Adelaide. I go where I'm told. The first race of the season is here and it's often stinking hot. They wanted race conditions.'

'Do you spend a lot of time here?'

'I've been coming here since I was twenty-two, every year for the past eight years, to race but I don't get to see a lot. We fly in, spend four days at the race track and have one rest day before heading to the next spot.'

'What's your favourite place of anywhere you've been?'

'Home,' he said. 'I always look forward to going home to the Coast, probably because I don't get to spend enough time there, but here is pretty good too.'

'Adelaide?'

'No. Right here. With you. At the risk of sounding like a crazy stalker, I asked the nurses to leave me at the kiosk because I was hoping I'd see you there.'

She smiled and he thought she seemed pleased. 'And what were you planning on doing if I didn't turn up?'

'I thought about hanging around the ICU but I didn't want to look completely crazy or desperate.'

She laughed. 'Probably a wise decision.'

'What about you?' he asked. 'Where is your favourite place?'

Ruby had been leaning on the railing at the edge of the lake, facing him. He'd had trouble concentrating as her thighs were level with his eyes and were proving to be very distracting. She pushed herself off the railing as she said, 'Come on, I'll show you.'

He frowned. 'It's here?'

'Yep.'

The path she chose took them past a small kiosk at the northern end of the lake. Chairs and tables were shaded by umbrellas and there were signs advertising ice cream.

'Hang on,' he said, when he saw the signs. 'How about I buy you that drink I owe you?'

She detoured past the kiosk counter. 'I wouldn't say no to a strawberry gelato.'

Somehow he'd known she would taste like strawberries.

He ordered strawberry for her and a coffee gelato for him.

'More coffee?'

'One of my vices,' he admitted. It wasn't something he was supposed to drink a lot of. Large quantities were considered incompatible with his occupation but he'd never been able to give it up completely.

'What are your other vices?' she asked, as they waited for their order.

'Fast cars.'

He knew she was waiting for him to say more. Sometimes he would quip about fast women but he wanted Ruby to think favourably of him. There was something different about her, something special, and it made him chose his words carefully. He didn't want to come across as flippant or careless. He hadn't been able to get her out of his head and he wanted to create a good impression.

'Don't eat it yet,' she admonished, as he attempted to dip the spoon into the gelato. 'Save it for a moment.'

He was happy to follow her direction. He was naturally right-handed and tasks that he'd never thought about were proving rather challenging when he had to rely on his left hand. He was happy to let the gelato soften a little more.

She pushed him up an inclined path towards a spectacular building perched on top of a hill. It was made almost entirely of glass. The central section had a huge domed ceiling and glass wings extended from either side and ended in curved glass walls. The panes of glass were clear, with the exception of some at the very top of the walls that were stained a peacock blue. The building must have stretched for fifty metres, if not further, and the summer sunlight bouncing off the glass made it look like a massive diamond.

'What is this place?'

'This is my favourite place.' She stepped around in front of his chair and waved one arm expansively towards it. 'It's the Palm House. Isn't it gorgeous?'

'It is,' he agreed.

Ruby's face was alight with pleasure. Her green eyes shone and he wished he had a camera to capture her expression.

'It might be a tad warm inside but we'll just stay a little while. Just long enough to eat our gelato,' she said as she wheeled him inside.

The floor was tiled in an intricate pattern of black, ochre and cream, and ornate plaster garden beds followed the curves of the building. Ruby pushed him along the tiled floor to the far end of one of the wings and tucked his chair into a little alcove, turning him so he had a view back along the central pathway. The path was lined with lush palms and the afternoon sun streamed through the glass walls and was filtered through the palm fronds.

Ruby sat on the cream plaster wall of the garden bed beside him and took an enormous scoop of her gelato. She tipped her head back and looked up at the domed glass ceiling as she sucked the gelato off the spoon. Her long, slim neck was exposed and he had a strong urge to kiss her throat, and then her mouth closed around the spoon while she slowly pulled the spoon out through her lips and he forgot all about her throat. All he could think about now were her lips. He watched, fascinated, as she ate her gelato.

The scoop she'd taken had been too big to eat all in one mouthful and the gelato that remained on the spoon had been moulded to the shape of the inside of her mouth. She put the spoon back into her mouth and sucked the rest of the gelato off it. He'd never seen anyone eat an ice cream that sensually before.

He could imagine the warmth of her mouth on his flesh as her lips closed around him and he felt a stirring in his groin as he watched her lick the spoon clean with a pointed pink tongue. It was good to know that some important parts of his anatomy hadn't been damaged in the accident.

He needed to adjust himself but it was hard to do when he only had one functioning hand and it was busy holding a cup of gelato. Some distraction was needed and he hoped conversation would suffice.

'What appeals to you about the palm house?' he asked. He was curious to hear her answer. The plants weren't the prettiest in the gardens, there were plenty of palms and a lot of dry-climate plants, the type that would maybe flower once a year, but they certainly weren't as beautiful or as sweet-smelling as others, but the building was stunning. He could understand if the building itself resonated with her. Ruby wasn't terribly forthcoming about herself. Perhaps finding out what made this spot important to her would give him some more insight into what made her tick.

She should have expected the question but she was caught unprepared with an answer. Perhaps she'd made a mistake, bringing him here. She feared her impulsiveness might make things awkward.

The palm house had been built in Germany in the nineteenth century and shipped out to Australia in pieces, before being reassembled in Adelaide. The plants it housed were from Madagascar. Ruby had always felt it was an odd combination, a European building filled with African plants and transplanted into an Australian garden, but somehow it worked and it gave her hope that even though she often felt out of place, maybe one day she too would find a place to belong. But she wasn't prepared to share those thoughts with Noah. Not at this point in time and probably not ever.

But Australia was filled with buildings that had their origins in other countries and the others didn't affect her in the same way. There was something more about this one. There was another reason why this building touched her soul and this reason she could share without revealing anything as personal.

'I love the idea that something made of glass, something so fragile and beautiful, can be strong and protective too. I love how it offers shelter to everything within it. I'd like to be like that.'

'You're not?'

'No. This building reminds me of Scarlett. My other sister.'

'The dark-haired one?' he asked.

Ruby nodded as she finished her gelato. 'She's the family protector. She's the one who always has our backs, she's the one we turn to in a crisis. I'd like to be strong like that but I'm not sure that I am.'

Noah was watching her closely. He didn't comment and she wondered if she'd made him feel uncomfortable, if she'd shared too much. She stood up from the wall. It was time to move on. If they were moving maybe neither of them would feel that they had to speak. She didn't want him to ask any questions that she couldn't answer. He had finished his ice cream and their hour was up. As much as she'd enjoyed their excursion, it was time to return him to the hospital before she gave away any more of her secrets.

Ruby was glad to have Rose to herself when she got back to the ICU. She needed some time to sort through what had just happened with Noah. For a big man there was a sense of calmness about him that lulled her into a state of peace and security, and his unwavering blue-eyed gaze and his quiet, deep voice made it seem as though he really was interested in her and what she had to say. She'd have to be careful. It was too easy to let her guard down around him.

He'd been able to make her laugh. He'd been able to make her forget about life's problems for a while. All she could think about when she was with him, all she wanted to think about, was how she could get him to smile for her. The only time she had laughed in the past four days had been when she had been with him.

It made no sense. To all intents and purposes he was a stranger but somehow she just knew he was going to be more than that. He was going to be important.

Ruby didn't bother picking up the novel from beside the bed. She had far better things to talk to Rose about today.

'I've just had the most amazing time,' she told her as she pushed the strands of blond hair from her sister's forehead and kissed her gently. 'Have you ever walked into a room and seen a man—he might not be the most handsome or the tallest or the best dressed—you know nothing about him, you don't know if he's nice or funny or smart because he's a complete stranger, but for some inexplicable reason your eyes meet and you are drawn together? There's an instant connection and you know he feels it too. How could he not?'

Ruby pulled a tube of hand cream from her bag and squeezed a dollop into her palm. She picked up Rose's hand and massaged the cream into her skin. It was a soothing gesture, one she hoped would calm Rose as much as it would her. Ruby had been running on adrenalin since meeting Noah. Her heart was still racing and she needed to stop and take a breath. She needed to stop and take stock of what had just happened.

'You know the expression "Their eyes met across a crowded room"?' she said, as she worked the cream into Rose's hand. 'I always thought that was just something people said, but it's true. We weren't exactly in a crowded room, not the first time, but the second time, in the hospital kiosk, it really felt as though we were the only two people there. It was incredible.

'I have no idea whether you've ever felt like that about someone, Rosie. I'm sorry I've never asked you but I hope, one day, you have this feeling too. This feeling that some things happen for a reason. Some things are just meant to be.'

It was easy to talk to Rose because she couldn't talk back. She couldn't ask any difficult questions and Ruby didn't have to feel self-conscious about these unfamiliar feelings.

'His name is Noah,' she continued, 'and he is the most gorgeous man. Handsome and nice, with the sexiest voice and a taste for adventure that, I admit, I find irresistible. There's something about him, Rose, that I can't ignore.

'I know you'd say I get carried away every time I meet someone new but Noah is different.

'Or maybe I am.'

She pondered that thought for a moment as she moved around the bed and began to massage Rose's other hand.

'Maybe I'm looking for something different, something more, and seeing it in Noah when it might not be there. You'd probably say I'm projecting but I can't deny how I felt when he held my hand. His skin was warm and his touch made the butterflies in my stomach take flight. And his smile just makes everything seem brighter. And have I told you about his eyes? He's got the most incredible eyes. That's where the connection is. He just has to look at me and I want to melt.

'He's exciting, Rosie. He makes me excited. He just has to look at me and I want him. And I'm going to have him, too. I have to.'

Ruby closed her eyes as she pictured Noah taking her into his arms. She could imagine running her fingers through his hair and over the rough stubble of his beard and feeling his arms around her. Feeling the heat of his body against hers and the beating of his heart.

She had always loved new beginnings, new possibilities, and a new relationship was no exception. She loved the feeling of an initial attraction, the excitement and anticipation. It was like having a fresh, clean slate. Like the beach in the early morning after the tide had gone out and there wasn't a mark on the sand until someone took that first step.

At the beginning of a relationship Ruby always felt

like the freshly washed sand. When the other person didn't know her very well she got a chance to create a new Ruby. She got a chance to draw lines in the sand until she had made the person she wanted someone else to see.

She loved the opportunity to start afresh. There was always the hope that if she got enough chances to re-invent herself then one day she just might get it right.

'Hi, Rubes. I'm glad you're here. Jake and I need to talk to you.'

Ruby opened her eyes as Scarlett's voice interrupted her daydreams.

'What's up?'

'We have to make a decision about the wedding,' Scarlett said, as she sank into the spare chair beside Rose's bed.

'What do you mean?'

'The wedding can't go ahead as we'd planned,' Jake explained. 'Rose won't be out of hospital by the weekend and if we're going to postpone the wedding I'll need to notify people and cancel the reception venue.'

'You're going to postpone it?'

'We're not sure. We can't decide.'

'That's why we thought we'd get your opinion. You can be the impartial umpire.'

Ruby wasn't sure she was up to that task. 'I don't know if I can make that call.'

'Just listen to the options and give us your opinion,' Scarlett asked her.

'I suggested that we have the ceremony here,' Jake told her.

'In the ICU?'

He nodded. 'With just the bare minimum of people. Us, you, your mum, Rose obviously and my parents. We can get married here and then have the reception as planned. The other guests can just join us for the party.'

Ruby couldn't see what was wrong with that plan if they were determined to get married, but from Scarlett's expression it seemed that plan wasn't her favourite. 'What do you think, Scarlett?' she asked her sister.

'I'm not really in the mood for a party and that's what the reception will be.'

'Okay, let's cancel the reception and just get married,' Jake suggested. 'Keep it simple.'

'I want to wait,' Scarlett told him. 'I want to marry you but I want both my sisters to be there when I do.'

'Rose *would* be there.'

Scarlett shook her head. 'I want her to be part of it. I want to give her a chance to get well. I don't care about a big white wedding, that's never been my dream, I would marry you in a registry office or in the hospital chapel, but I want Ruby and Rose standing beside me.'

Ruby wasn't sure why they needed her opinion. If someone wanted to wait, wasn't that what you did? But she could tell that Jake was worried about what would happen if Rose didn't make it and she knew that was why he didn't want to delay but, to his credit, he didn't voice that thought.

'What do you reckon, Rubes?' Scarlett asked.

She wanted to tell them they should get married and that Rose would understand but she couldn't do it. She didn't actually believe that. She took a deep breath.

'If I were in Rose's shoes I'd want you to wait. I'm sorry, I know that probably sounds selfish but that's my opinion. Rose has made it through four days, she *will* get better. We have to believe that. Can you wait? Just long enough to give her a chance to wake up?'

'Please, Jake.' Scarlett held his hands as she pleaded with him. 'As soon as she's awake we'll get married, I promise.'

Jake nodded and smiled. 'Okay, I'm not going to argue with two of you. You're right, we'll wait for Rose.'

Scarlett threw her arms around his neck and kissed him. 'Thank you. I love you.'

'I love you too. You know I just want you to have a perfect wedding.'

Ruby wondered what they would do if things didn't go according to plan but she figured Jake would work something out. He seemed to know how to handle Scarlett. She was obviously the most important person in his life and his mission seemed to be to take care of her and keep her happy and he was apparently doing a good job of both.

Ruby wished again that she had someone like Jake in her life. Someone who would put her first. Someone who she knew would always be there for her.

Thursday, 18th December

Thursday looked as though it was going to be a very ordinary day. Ruby had been so confident yesterday that things were improving for Rose. She'd been convinced that Rose had turned the corner. She'd made it through four days—surely that counted for something— but someone had apparently forgotten to tell the doctors the good news and they had a different perspective to Ruby and she didn't like what they told her. She had to

admit it wasn't all *bad* news but what she didn't understand was why it couldn't be all *good* news.

She hated herself for not coping. She hated knowing
she wasn't strong enough to deal with this but that didn't
change the fact that it was true.

She had to get away from the ICU. She needed some
time and space to work out why she was so upset.

She paced the hospital corridors until, once again,
she found herself outside Noah's room. That was no
surprise. For the past two days she had felt best when
she'd been with him. She couldn't explain why that was,
she still hadn't quite been able to work out what it was
about him that made her feel better—all she knew was
that he brightened her day.

Was it his rebellious streak, his taste for adventure
that made her feel she could escape from the real world
when she was with him?

Was it his sense of capability and control? He was
gorgeous and big and she got a sense that he could and
would protect her. Even though she knew that was a ridiculous notion at the moment, given that he was being
held together by metal rods and slings and painkillers,
but he still seemed capable of anything.

Was it the fact he was able to make her laugh, something she needed badly at this point in time?

Or was it his smile and his warm blue eyes that fixed
her under his spell?

She pushed open his door, hoping her timing was
good and he'd had his daily physio and would be happy
for her company.

'Ruby!' His obvious pleasure turned to concern.
'What's wrong? Is it Rose?'

Maybe it was simply the sense that he knew her already? He'd taken one look at her and had somehow known she was upset. How did he know her so well? Did he feel that same connection?

Ruby could feel her emotions building. Tears were threatening but she couldn't have said whether they were being caused by Noah's concern or by her own concern for her sister. She nodded.

'What's happened? Is it bad news?'

'Not completely,' she sniffed, fighting back tears. 'She's responding to the antibiotics, the rash isn't spreading and the septicaemia is under control. They're going to lighten the sedation so she'll gradually wake up and be weaned off the life support.'

'That sounds like good news to me.'

'It's mostly good news but they are also talking about the possibility that they may have to amputate some of her toes and they're worried about her kidney function too.'

'So things aren't perfect but could they still be worse?'

'Yes, but I don't want them to be worse, I want them to be better.' She knew she sounded spoilt and self-indulgent but she couldn't help how she felt. She tried to explain her feelings more succinctly. 'You're right, things could be a lot worse, and I know I'm being silly, but all our lives we've been defined a certain way and I don't want things to change.'

'Defined how?'

'Scarlett is the clever one, Rose is the pretty one...'

'And you are?'

'I'm supposed to be the fun one. But I'm not feeling very fun today,' she admitted. Ruby did like to have fun. If people saw her having fun she thought they wouldn't notice that she was lonely. And by going out and having fun she made sure she had company. It was a win-win situation. 'And I don't want Rose to have scars.'

'You said she *may* need surgery so if, and I'll say it again, *if,* she needs that surgery, it's only toes, it won't change the way she looks. She'll still be pretty. I think you, on the other hand, need to get out of here and have some fun. I will take charge today, as long as you agree to push me wherever I decide to go. We need to get out into the real world. You need to be kept busy.'

Ruby was happy to let Noah take control. She didn't feel like being in charge today. He signed himself out and then directed her to the cosmopolitan hub of Rundle Street, one block to the south. A two-block strip of fashion boutiques, coffee shops and pubs, it was busy with the lunchtime crowd. The street was festooned with Christmas decorations and the boutique windows showcased a colourful display of party dresses for the festive season. Ruby had never felt less like celebrating Christmas and, once again, her circumstances meant that the holiday had completely slipped her mind.

'That would look nice on you.'

She paused in front of a shop window when Noah pointed out a stunning dress on the display. It was a simple black dress and she could imagine how it would look on her. She had very similar proportions to display mannequins, long, thin limbs and no boobs worth mentioning, but the dress had been cleverly, and heavily, beaded, which created the illusion of a figure that was far curvier than hers. The figure of a woman. Her fair skin was a good foil for black and Ruby thought Noah was right—the style probably would suit her—but she had never owned anything as beautiful as this and she couldn't imagine wearing it.

'Where would I ever wear it? It's not really the thing for Byron Bay, it's far too fancy.' Byron Bay wasn't known for its formality and Ruby didn't really enjoy shopping. She bought clothes from thrift shops, knowing that the money was going to a good cause, and when she moved, as she was often wont to do, she donated the clothes back. They were only clothes after all. She looked at the dress and knew it would cost more than her entire wardrobe put together. 'It's far too beautiful for me.'

'I disagree.'

Did he really think she was pretty enough to wear that dress? He was looking at her so intently that she almost believed him but his attention embarrassed her so she took off again, pushing him in front of her, avoiding his eyes as she searched for a table that could accommodate them for a coffee.

There were crowds of people sitting at sidewalk tables, enjoying a glass of wine with lunch or a beer at one of the several pubs in the street, but she continued past them all. Noah shouldn't drink in his condition so she didn't feel like she should offer to stop. The crowd sitting outside the Exeter Hotel was particularly boisterous and caught Noah's attention.

'Shall I buy you a drink?' he offered. 'Would a glass of wine be a good stress-reliever?'

Ruby shook her head. 'I don't drink alcohol,' she told him.

'You don't? Why not?' He sounded surprised but Ruby was used to that reaction.

'I don't like the way it makes me feel.' That was a half-truth. The rest of the story was that she'd made a few bad decisions when she'd been drinking, actually more than a few, but she wasn't going to elaborate. That was definitely not a conversation she planned on having with Noah. She parked him at the next empty café table they came across and went inside to order, hoping that would be enough to end the discussion.

'Are you feeling better yet?' Noah asked, as she poured herself a second cup of green tea from the pot.

'Not really.' She sighed. 'It's been a big twenty-four hours since I saw you yesterday.'

In just a couple of days spending time with Noah had become a good foil for the time spent in ICU. Time spent worrying about Rose, time spent getting nowhere, time spent on edge around her mother was counteracted by Noah's ability to relax her, to make her laugh and to let her think about other things, but he wasn't having his usual influence on her today.

'Something else is bothering you?' he asked.

Ruby knew she wasn't being great company and she owed it to Noah to explain why. 'Scarlett and Jake were supposed to be getting married this weekend but they've had to postpone the wedding.'

'Because of Rose?'

Ruby nodded.

'You don't agree with their decision?'

'No, I do. They want to wait until Rose is better, or at least conscious, which I think is the right thing to do… But it means that I will need to stay in Adelaide longer, which means I need to find somewhere to live.' That was the crux of the matter. It was another issue that she had to deal with but, once again, she didn't know where to start.

'I'm not following you. Where are you living now?'

'At Scarlett's, but I want to give them some privacy and I can't afford to stay in a hotel.'

'Why don't you stay with your mother?'

'I can't stay with Lucy, we clash too much, we always have, and it's not good for anyone and especially not at the moment. We're all under enough stress, without adding living arrangements into the mix.'

'What about a friend? You said you had friends who worked at the hospital.'

'I may have exaggerated a little.'

Noah smiled as Ruby continued.

'I left Adelaide when I was sixteen. I haven't lived here for ten years and I lost touch with my friends. I do have one friend who is a nurse at the hospital but she and her husband haven't been married all that long and that would make me feel more uncomfortable than staying with Scarlett.'

Ruby realised that for the first time since they'd met they had talked more about her than about him. She'd forgotten his talent for turning the conversation back to her and she'd forgotten to be careful. She still wasn't sure why she found herself telling him her story. She never talked about herself. Never. She'd only intended to tell him about the wedding and here she was, talking to him about her past.

Noah was silent for a little bit. He finished his coffee, also in silence, and Ruby started to worry that she'd said too much.

'Can you cook?' he asked, as he put his cup down.

Ruby frowned. 'What?'

'Cooking—are you any good at it?'

'I'm okay.' Pasta and stir fries counted as cooking, didn't they?

'I have a suggestion for you, then.'

'Really?' Ruby couldn't imagine what he could suggest. Or what cooking had to do with anything.

'I need a nurse-cum-housekeeper.'

'You do? What on earth for?'

'My racing team have rented a furnished apartment, it was where I was staying before the accident put me in hospital. The hospital has agreed to discharge me, which means I can go back to the apartment, but I won't be able to manage on my own. I've got one good arm and it's my left one, which isn't particularly useful when I'm right-handed, and I've got one good leg. I won't be able to use crutches for a few weeks so I'm stuck in this chair. I need some help with general tasks, cooking and showering and the like, and it makes sense if I can have one person who can do it all. Craig, the team manager, was going to arrange some agency help but I'd prefer it if it was you.'

'Me?'

'It makes sense, doesn't it? I already know you and you're a nurse. The apartment has plenty of room. The team would pay you a wage and the arrangement would give you somewhere to live. If you don't mind being a nurse and cook. The apartment is on the other side of the south parklands, only a few minutes from the hospital. It would still be convenient for you in terms of visiting Rose as well.

'Why don't you think about it and let me know tomorrow? As soon as I've got some help organised, I can get out of here.'

She didn't need to think about it. If someone else got the job she wouldn't have any reason to see him again. He would be out of hospital and out of her life. And she didn't want that. There were probably half a dozen reasons why this was a bad idea but she couldn't think of any at present. All she could think of was one very good reason to do this—she would be able to keep seeing Noah.

'I'll do it.'

It was an easy decision. She just hoped it was the right one.

CHAPTER FIVE

Friday, 19th December

'You're doing what?'

Scarlett's reaction shouldn't have surprised Ruby. The role of sensible older sister, who looked out for everyone else, came naturally to her, but Ruby hadn't really expected her announcement to be a big deal. To Ruby the arrangement made perfect sense in every way.

'I'm going to be a live-in nurse.'

'For a man you've just met?'

'It's a job, Scarlett. I need somewhere to live and I need an income. This works for me.'

'But you don't know anything about him!'

'I know enough, as much as I would about any client. If he was eighty-five and infirm you wouldn't be carrying on like this, would you?'

'But he's not, is he?'

'No.' Ruby grinned. 'He's seriously hot. It's much more fun that way,' she teased.

Scarlett rolled her eyes and turned to Candice. 'Have you met him?' she asked.

'No, but all reports seem to agree with Ruby. Apparently he's gorgeous and he's loaded and he's nice.'

Candice shrugged. 'As a nurse, I can think of plenty of worse jobs than being Noah Christiansen's live-in carer.'

Ruby knew Scarlett had called in reinforcements to lend weight to her argument but it seemed as though her plan to invite Candice to join them for dinner might have backfired.

'But I don't understand why you have to live in.' Scarlett wasn't giving up easily. 'You can stay with us.'

'Scarlett, really, be logical. I appreciate the offer but I'm not going to stay with you. You're supposed to be on your honeymoon, you're seven and a half months pregnant and Jake is about to start his internship. You've got enough to deal with.'

'Well, if you need somewhere to live and someone to look after, you could move back in with Mum and Rose. I'm sure Mum could use some help.'

Ruby felt a little bit guilty. She had fully intended to pull her weight, to grow up and take some responsibility, and yet what was she doing? At the first opportunity she was bailing. 'You know how that would end,' she protested. 'I can't move back in with Mum. I left when I was sixteen and I'm not going back now. I can still help with Rose once she's out of hospital. I can take her to appointments or whatever, I'll just have to juggle things.'

Scarlett turned to Candice, who, in Ruby's opinion, seemed to have the good sense to stay out of the argument. 'You and Ewan have a spare room, don't you?'

'Scarlett, stop,' Ruby interrupted. 'I've made my decision.'

'You've got to stop running, Ruby.'

She knew she'd eventually have to learn to deal with things but she couldn't make herself do it just yet. It was much easier to run off with Noah. But at least she

was planning on staying in town. 'I'm not running,' she
argued. 'Noah will need help for a while and this gives
me something to do and somewhere to stay while Rose
recovers and until you and Jake can get married.'

Noah was her escape from the stress and drama of
her family and, while she knew she was taking the easy
option, she had no intention of changing her mind. But
she was prepared to extend Scarlett an olive branch. 'If
it will make you feel any better, you can meet him be-
forehand,' she offered, assuming that Scarlett would be
too preoccupied with other matters to take her up on
this suggestion.

Saturday, 20th December

'Noah?'

His hospital door opened and an attractive woman
with dark hair stepped into his room. 'I'm—'

He had been expecting Ruby and this definitely
wasn't her, but he recognised her anyway. 'Scarlett,'
he interrupted.

A frown appeared between the woman's dark eyes.
'How do you know who I am?'

'I remember you from the ICU. It's a pleasure to meet
you.'

'I wanted to talk to you—'

'About Ruby,' he interrupted again.

'Yes.'

Scarlett shut the door and Noah started to laugh.

'What's so funny?' she asked.

'Ruby warned me to expect you and I've been wondering how long it would take before you came to check
me out and make sure I'm not a crazy serial killer. Even

if I didn't remember you from the ICU, you're just like Ruby described. Am I right in assuming you want to know what my intentions are?'

Scarlett folded her arms and rested them on her pregnant belly. 'Something like that.'

'I promise everything is above board and totally legitimate. I've got some major rehab ahead of me if I want to get back to work in the foreseeable future. I'm not going to make it if I'm stuck in here for any length of time. Ruby told me you're a doctor, you know getting out of here will be the best thing for my recovery,' he said, hoping to appeal to her practical side, 'but in order to get discharged, I need some help. I'm not kidnapping Ruby, I'm not taking advantage of her, I'm not sleeping with her, I'm employing her. As my carer.'

'Does she know that?'

'Yes. This was her decision and she is an adult.'

'She doesn't always act like one.'

'Ruby told me she hasn't lived here for ten years. She must have managed to run her life without any help while she's been away.'

Scarlett's expression made Noah think that maybe that wasn't the case. He wondered what had gone wrong in the past. *Intriguing.*

He had seen Ruby retreat into her shell on several occasions but although he was gradually learning more about her it was all in bits and pieces and he had suspected she was deliberately withholding information. Scarlett's expression confirmed his suspicions and further piqued his curiosity.

He knew she didn't drink alcohol but she hadn't really explained why. Likewise, she'd told him she'd moved away at the age of sixteen but had told him nothing further. He'd have to remember to ask her where she'd gone when she'd left and find out what she'd been up to for the past ten years. Sixteen was young to move away, unless her whole family had gone, but he had the distinct impression that hadn't been the case.

He'd have plenty of opportunity to learn everything he could about her—they were about to spend a lot of time together. He was excited about that. She fascinated him.

'She's a bit vulnerable at the moment.' The warning note in Scarlett's words was evident. 'She doesn't cope well with stress.'

'And you're not sure that she's thinking clearly?' He agreed she was going through a stressful time but he thought she was coping remarkably well. Most people would find the week Ruby had just had stressful and it was his opinion that Ruby knew exactly what she was doing. He thought that she coped better with life than other people, for whatever reason, liked to believe.

'Don't you think it's strange that she's jumped at this chance when she knows nothing about you?'

'It's a job, nothing more,' he said, hoping he wouldn't be caught out in a lie, but at this stage that was all it was. Scarlett didn't need to know anything else, not yet. 'I can't manage on my own—I need someone to give me a hand and Ruby needs somewhere to stay. This made sense—to both of us.'

'She's doesn't need a place to stay,' Scarlett argued. 'She can stay with me.'

'She doesn't want to.' Noah wasn't about to back down, it wasn't in his nature. Scarlett might have her opinion but he had one too and he was never afraid of a challenge. 'She wants to give you some space, as I'm sure she's told you. I'm not denying it suits me to have Ruby look after me but it suits her too.'

Monday, 22nd December

It was the beginning of a new week and Ruby had a feeling things were going to improve. The doctors were beginning to wean Rose from the ventilator. Her sedation had been lightened gradually over the past few days and there had been definite signs she was waking up. Her blood gases were good and everyone, Ruby included, was feeling extremely optimistic and positive about the outcome, and when Ruby stopped into the ICU and saw Rose's eyes were open she knew she'd been right.

'Rose! You're awake!' She turned to Lucy, who was sitting beside Rose, holding her hand while the nurse recorded her obs. 'Why didn't anyone call me?'

'The doctors were just doing a trial to see if she could breathe on her own,' Lucy told her. 'She did so well they decided to take her off the ventilator but they've only just removed it. There hasn't been time to call anyone yet.'

'How are you feeling?' Ruby asked, as she bent over to kiss Rose.

'Weird.' Rose's voice was raspy.

'You sound like me.' Ruby smiled.

'I know I've been here a week and I can remember some things but I don't know what happened when. I remember you reading to me. I liked that.'

Ruby felt a twinge of guilt. The only reason she hadn't given up reading initially had been because Noah had asked her to continue. If he hadn't, she might have closed the book and left it at that, and Rose wouldn't have that memory.

'And I remember Noah.'

'You do?'

'You made him sound hard to forget.'

The nurse interrupted them as she spoke to Rose. 'Your respiratory muscles will get tired easily,' she said. 'I'd suggest you keep conversation to a minimum for today and just concentrate on breathing again. Your muscles need to become fit.'

'It's okay,' Ruby replied. 'I'll do the talking for us both.' Today was the day she was going to start her new job as Noah's carer. She was looking forward to it, probably far more than she ought to and certainly far more than she would admit to anyone, but she couldn't keep the note of excitement out of her voice as she filled Rose in on what she'd missed.

'He gets discharged soon,' she said, as she checked the time. 'And then it will be your turn next.' Ruby was convinced now that Rose would get out of here too. 'I'd better go but I'll see you later, okay?'

Ruby left Rose and Lucy and made her way down to Noah's ward. He was ready and waiting. She accompanied Noah, the nurse who was responsible for his discharge and Craig Bellamy, Noah's team manager, out of the hospital. It was quite a procession but in a few minutes Ruby and Noah would be on their own. Noah's discharge would be complete and Ruby would be responsible for his well-being. She was on an emotional high. Her day couldn't be going any better.

Craig had been busy organising all the things Ruby had thought she might need to manage Noah's care, including transport. 'The car is this way,' he said, as he led them through the car park.

Ruby's heart plummeted when Craig pushed the button to unlock the car and she heard the 'beep beep' and saw the corresponding flash of the indicator lights.

'No way! I can't drive a racing car!'

The car was completely covered in writing and company logos from the front fender to the back bumper bar. Ruby wasn't a particularly confident driver and this was definitely a 'look at me' type of car. There was no chance she could drive through the streets inconspicuously in this. She didn't want to draw attention to herself but there'd be no way to avoid it in this vehicle.

'It's just an ordinary car,' Noah replied. 'The paintwork is just part of our sponsorship deal, it's only advertising.'

'And you were worried about being seen in those sunglasses I bought you from the gift shop?' Ruby said, as she checked it out.

'I get paid to wear glasses from a certain designer. I was more worried that someone would recognise me and think the designer had lost his touch,' Noah explained with a smile, as Craig opened the passenger side door.

'Well, I'm not sure that having me behind the wheel is going to be good for your image or your sponsors either,' Ruby said, when she looked inside.

'Why not?'

'It's a manual.' She hadn't thought to ask for an automatic, she'd never imagined the car would have a manual gearbox.

'Can't you drive a manual?'

'I can but not very well. It's years since I've had to. I assumed it would be an automatic.'

'I can arrange something else but it will take a few hours,' Craig offered.

Ruby shrugged. Her day was going rapidly downhill

but she wasn't going to let a few minor problems dampen her mood. She'd have to cope. 'It's all right, I'll give it a go.' She turned to Noah and added the proviso, 'As long as you're prepared to take the risk?'

'I make my living speeding around a race circuit with twenty other cars all travelling in excess of two hundred kilometres per hour and all jockeying for the same position. You can't be as dangerous as that!'

The sound of his laughter bolstered her enthusiasm and she grinned. 'You'd think not, so let's hope I don't surprise you.'

With the nurse's assistance Noah transferred from the hospital wheelchair into the car as Craig opened the boot and ran through some final details with Ruby.

'The electric wheelchair is disassembled and is in here. Will you be all right to put it together?'

'I should be able to work that out,' she said. She didn't want Craig to think she was completely useless, he might decide not to employ her. Noah had asked for an electric wheelchair and they'd decided that with left-hand controls he should be able to operate it and this would give him a bit of independence, at least around the apartment.

'Most of Noah's things are already there and I've had the rest of the equipment you requested delivered to the penthouse too. Here is a credit card for your use, the details are inside here, and these are the access cards for the apartment. I think that's it,' Craig said, as he handed her a large yellow envelope.

Ruby took a deep breath as she slid into the driver's seat. This was it. They were alone. For the next few weeks she and Noah would be almost inseparable. She was both eager and terrified. She was excited at the prospect but nervous that the experience wasn't going to live up to her expectations. She glanced across at Noah. He grinned at her, his blue eyes full of mischief, as she turned the key in the ignition. She relaxed. She was pretty sure she was going to enjoy the next month or two.

She put the car into gear and somehow managed not to stall the engine, but she didn't give the car quite enough fuel and she bunny-hopped out of the parking lot and around the East End, much to Noah's amusement.

She wasn't sure she liked the sound of his laugh quite so much when he was laughing at her expense. 'You might not be laughing after a few days of this,' she told him.

'You don't think you'll improve?'

'One can only hope,' she said, as she flicked the indicator on and turned left through the parklands. 'Oh, hell.'

'What's wrong?'

'I didn't mean to come this way. I've always hated this roundabout,' she said, as the notorious Britannia roundabout loomed ahead of them.

'Get in the right-hand lane and hug the roundabout,' he told her. 'That way it won't matter what the other cars do, you'll be out of their way.'

But even with the new dual roundabout system Ruby made hard work of it. Another car cut across in front of her and she slammed on the brakes and just avoided stalling the engine. That rattled her and she almost missed the exit, but eventually she was through safely and in a couple of minutes Noah was directing her into the car park under the apartment block.

Ruby swiped the card that let them access the lift to the penthouse and tried, unsuccessfully, not to act like a country bumpkin when the doors slid open and she stepped straight into an apartment that could have come from the pages of a glossy high-end interiors magazine. Noah had already mastered control of the electric wheelchair and she let him go in front of her, glad he couldn't see the stunned expression on her face.

The apartment was superb. The polished floors of the foyer led into an open-plan kitchen, living and dining room. The kitchen was built for entertaining with a massive granite island bench, an industrial range hood, a double oven and a state-of-the-art coffee machine that Ruby suspected she'd never work out.

Modular leather lounges were clustered in front of floor-to-ceiling windows that looked out onto an enormous balcony with views from the hills to the city and out to the coast. The living and dining area were separated by a pod-shaped wood fire, which was suspended from the ceiling, and a baby grand piano was tucked into the corner of the room. Ruby had never seen anything quite like it before. The apartment was luxurious, expensive, modern and stunning.

Fortunately, it was single level, with the bedrooms positioned on the opposite side of the living room. The main bedroom had city views and a small en suite bathroom, which was not designed to accommodate Noah's chair. He insisted that Ruby take the main bedroom and he would take the room across the hall. Ruby quelled her disappointment at the idea of separate bedrooms. What had she expected? That he would want to jump straight into bed with her? He really wasn't in any state to be fooling around. Not yet. She tried to concentrate as they finished the tour and Noah gave her a lesson in how to work the coffee machine.

Once he'd had his caffeine fix he was ready to move on to other business. He took a whiteboard marker from one of the kitchen drawers and handed it to Ruby. 'Can I ask you to draw up a calendar on one of the windows?'

'A calendar?'

Noah nodded. 'I need somewhere to record my weekly goals and rehab plans, including my daily exercise routine and appointments.'

Ruby looked at the enormous, and spotlessly clean, window. He wanted her to write on that!? 'Why do you want to put it up here?' she asked. 'Why don't you just save all this into your phone? I can do that for you if you like.'

'I want a constant reminder of where I'm at and where I need to get to,' he explained. 'And if you have to drive me to my appointments it'll be easier if we can both see what's happening at a glance. I need you to write it because if I do it left-handed neither of us will be able to read it.'

Ruby shrugged and started drawing squares on the windows and writing the date in little numbers in the top left-hand corner of each.

He stopped her when she reached the fourteenth of February.

'Why are you finishing there?' She was positive he'd told her the racing season started at the end of the month—it was the same time as Scarlett's baby was due, which was why she'd remembered it—but Noah's home-made calendar was finishing two weeks earlier. 'I thought you said the first race wasn't until the end of Feb?'

'It isn't but there's a test day in Sydney on the fourteenth. The teams get out on the race track to test the cars. That's my goal. I need to be fit for that weekend if I'm to have any chance of starting the season. I'll have to undergo a fitness test prior to that so that's what I'm aiming for.'

Ruby did a quick calculation. 'But that'll only be nine weeks since your accident.'

'I admit I might be pushing uphill to make it back but if I want to keep my spot on the team then that's my goal. I need to keep focused.'

'All right, then, what needs to go up here?'

'I've got a physio appointment tomorrow morning at ten-thirty. There'll be physio three times a week and you'll have to help me with daily exercises here. I have fortnightly specialist appointments, first one on the twenty-ninth of this month, and I'll have X-rays every four weeks. I'm hoping that after the next lot of X-rays I'll be allowed out of this chair and onto crutches. My elbow and collarbone should be able to take some weight by then.

'Can you make a note to remind me to speak to the physio to see if I can hire some Pilates equipment to use here? And hopefully I can get into the pool sooner rather than later for supported exercises.'

'Did the specialist tell you when you might expect to be able to weight-bear through your right leg?'

'No, that will depend on the X-rays, but as soon as I get the okay we can order an exercise bike or maybe I'll just use the gym here.'

'There's a gym?'

'Yes. A gym, an outdoor pool, an indoor pool, a spa, sauna, tennis court and a small cinema. We can go on a tour a bit later.'

Ruby couldn't imagine ever wanting to use the gym, she hated gyms with a passion, but she didn't mind swimming, although it sounded as though she'd have very little free time. Looking after Noah was sounding as though it was going to be the full-time job she had been employed for.

'So Pilates, pool exercises, cycling and gym work? How fit do you need to be?'

'It's not so much normal aerobic fitness. It's not sprint fitness, I need strength and endurance. The focus is on strengthening my core, back, legs, arms, but I also need endurance as the races can take up to three hours and my heart rate will sit between one seventy and two hundred beats per minute for the entire race.'

If her job was to help him to achieve his goals, she needed to pay attention. 'What do you need strength for?'

'It takes eighty kilograms of force to depress the brake pedal, twenty kilos to turn the steering-wheel and twenty-five kilograms to change gear. I might change gear twelve hundred times in a race. Core strength helps produce those forces and also helps me to absorb all the bumps and vibrations and cope with the G forces.'

Ruby couldn't believe he knew all these facts and figures off the top of his head. 'What is your normal exercise routine?'

'In pre-season, which is now, I'd train six days a week. Four gym sessions, two Pilates sessions and four endurance sessions, either a swim, a ride or a run. During the season I'll cut back. There'd be two rest days, usually Thursday and Monday, which are either side of an event, and then three race days, Friday, Saturday and Sunday, which only leaves a couple of days to fit in a gym session and then a Pilates session, followed with some cardio. I'm normally at home in Queensland for pre-season but obviously the accident has thrown a spanner in the works so I'll have to work extra hard to get fit in time for the first race.'

It was no wonder he looked as good as he did, she thought. He spent all his spare time exercising.

'There's only so much you can do,' Ruby told him. 'Your bones need time to heal.'

Noah shrugged. 'I was pretty fit before the accident, not quite peak fitness but close, so I'm hoping that will help to speed up my recovery. I just need to progress my rehab as quickly as I can. If I don't recover fast enough I'll be replaced, and I'm determined to give myself every chance to be back behind the wheel for the beginning of the season.'

Ruby wasn't about to argue about his fitness. He certainly looked like a man in peak physical condition—at least he did if you ignored his injuries. But her nursing training told her that he had a monumental task ahead of him but there was no denying he had the right attitude and even she was starting to believe that he might just pull this off. Although there was one thing he hadn't mentioned.

'What about driving practice?' she asked.

'None of us actually do that much driving in the off season so I can really just focus on rehab. You can exercise with me,' he suggested. 'It's always nicer to have company.'

Ruby laughed. 'I refuse to exercise,' she told him. 'Unless it's dancing or swimming, and I enjoy those things so they don't count. Don't expect me to run.'

'I won't be running anywhere for the moment either. Have you tried Pilates? You might like that.'

She wasn't sure about Pilates either. She'd rather have sex, and lots of it, but now was probably not the time to tell Noah that. 'We'll see,' was all she said.

CHAPTER SIX

Tuesday, 23rd December

EVERYTHING WAS TAKING a bit longer than Ruby had anticipated this morning and she wasn't sure if it was because she was tired or whether she was just out of practice with this side of nursing. She'd been doing agency work in a teenage drug and alcohol counselling centre in Byron Bay but she hadn't told Noah that in case he'd decided she wasn't the right person for this job. And she'd desperately wanted this job.

But she had tossed and turned for the better part of the night—she couldn't blame her bed, it was made up with soft linens, plump pillows and it was huge and comfortable but with far too much room for one person—she hadn't been able to stop thinking about Noah asleep in his own huge bed across the hall. He'd fallen sleep in front of the television and she'd woken him to put him to bed still dressed in his shorts and T-shirt. If he hadn't been so exhausted from the transfer from the hospital and so badly injured she would have been tempted to climb into bed with him. It had been sexual frustration that had kept her awake until the early hours of the morning but there was nothing she could do about that yet. She'd just have to be patient.

Noah was waiting for a shower and it was her job to help him. That was what she was being paid for, not to fantasise about getting into bed with him, but undressing him did nothing to deter her imagination.

Ruby wheeled him into the main bathroom before carefully removing his shirt. It was the first time she'd seen him shirtless since the ICU and he looked every bit as good as she remembered. She tried not to stare but she did take her time pulling his T-shirt over his head, which gave her a chance to check him out unobserved.

He had no body fat and his torso was smooth and trim with well-defined pectorals and abdominal muscles, but his arms were to die for. She was desperate to run her hands from his shoulders down over his biceps and forearms all the way to his fingers.

She chatted away as she removed his boxer shorts and helped him to transfer to the shower chair. She tried telling herself he was just like any other patient and to stop feasting her eyes on him but it was difficult to do. Every part of him was oversized and glorious. His skin was smooth, and while his arms and legs were lightly covered with blond hair his trunk was hair-free except for a narrow trail of fair hair that ran south from his navel. Ruby averted her eyes, afraid she'd be caught out, as she settled him into the shower chair before removing his sling.

She ran the shower and adjusted the temperature then pushed the shower chair under the flow of water. Noah was able to take care of most of his ablutions using his left hand but Ruby needed to help him with his left side and his hair. But as she stood behind him to wash his hair she realised that the maxi-dress she'd thrown on that morning to combat the forecast heat of the day was not the most suitable attire. She hadn't considered the logistics of the bathroom when she'd dressed. It was spacious with ultramodern fittings.

That was good because the shower chair had rolled easily behind the floor-to-ceiling frameless glass shower screen but the shower head was enormous and the water poured from it like a waterfall. It was nothing like the hospital showers and there was no way she was going to be able to wash him and stay out of the spray.

Noah's hair was thick and long and it took ages just to get the water to penetrate the strands. She squeezed shampoo into the palm of her hand and worked it through his hair, massaging it into his scalp. Noah closed his eyes and she felt him relax under her touch. Ruby took that as an invitation to feast her eyes on his perfect proportions as she washed his hair. She tipped his head backwards to rinse the shampoo out. His eyes remained closed and she was tempted to run her fingers over the planes of his face. His lips were slightly parted, which made it look as if he was waiting to be kissed. She wondered what he'd taste like. Coffee, she suspected.

Rivulets of water were running down his chest, coursing between his pectoral muscles and gathering along his sternum. Ruby watched transfixed as the water made its way towards his stomach. He had dropped the washcloth in his lap, protecting his modesty, but Ruby's eyes didn't need to travel any further, she didn't need to see what lay beneath the cloth, she had the perfect image captured in her memory. By the time she had finished rinsing his hair she was soaking wet and more than slightly aroused. She needed to gather herself together.

'All done,' she said, as she flicked off the water and pushed him out of the shower. She exchanged the wet washcloth in his lap for a towel and used a second towel to dry him off. She stood behind him to dry his hair, squeezing the water from it before moving around to stand in front of him to dry his arms and chest. Her wet dress clung to her breasts, stomach and thighs, leaving little to the imagination, and she could see him looking at her as she leant over him. Her temperature rose steadily as he devoured her with his eyes.

She dropped her gaze and her hands. Her head dipped as she dried his stomach. Her head was aligned with his. He was close enough to kiss. All she needed to do was lean in a fraction more. She wanted him to close the gap. She wanted him to kiss her.

He lifted his head. She met his eyes. They had darkened considerably as his pupils dilated. He put his hand over hers, stilling her movements. She waited to feel his lips on hers but he moved no further.

'I can manage this bit,' he said. He took over, drying himself from the waist down.

She waited for him to finish before helping him to put his arm back into the sling. She leant over him, fiddling with the straps. She could feel his breath on her cheek. She lifted her eyes. His lips were millimetres away, tempting and teasing her.

She still wanted him to kiss her but instead she put her arms around him and helped him to stand.

They stood, hip to hip, chest to chest. Noah was locked in her embrace. They were as close as lovers.

Ruby's nipples were erect, reacting to the dampness of her dress and the sensation of Noah's body pressed up against hers. She could feel her nipples brushing his chest. She was aroused and she could feel he was too.

She looked up at him and met his blue-eyed gaze and this time when their eyes met he didn't hesitate. He dipped his head and claimed her for himself.

Ruby met him halfway, opening her mouth under the pressure of his lips, giving in to desire. She held on to him a little tighter, wrapping her arms a little more firmly around his back, her hands pressed into his shoulder blades as she fought to maintain their balance as their kiss deepened.

He tasted just like she'd imagined. Soft, warm and sweet, with faint traces of his morning coffee. She pressed her hands a little harder into his shoulder blades, trying to bring him closer as he cupped her bottom with his left hand and locked them together. Her knees felt like jelly and she wasn't sure who was supporting who.

Noah broke first.

'I have to sit down.'

Five simple words were enough to jolt her back to reality. And the reality was that he was badly injured and needed all his concentration to keep his balance while standing on one leg.

While she knew the attraction was mutual, the bottom line was that he wasn't physically capable of taking this any further. Yet.

'Sorry.'

'Don't be sorry.' He grinned as he lowered himself into the wheelchair. 'You should be thankful. If I was fully fit you wouldn't be able to keep up. If you start exercising now, you might be able to handle me.'

Ruby raised an eyebrow as she dropped a towel into his lap. The towel concealed his erection but Ruby was pleased to see from his reaction that she affected him as much as he did her. 'Is that a challenge?' she asked.

'If you want it to be. But it's only fair to warn you that I love a challenge.'

'Is that right?'

She was shivering now but she knew the goose bumps on her arms were more likely to be caused by the look in Noah's eyes than by her wet dress. But that didn't matter. If he wanted a challenge she'd give him one. She was eager to see how he coped with her next move.

She grabbed the skirt of her maxi-dress and turned her back to him as she pulled her dress over her head. She wasn't wearing a bra, she rarely did, but she kept her back turned towards him, giving him an eyeful of naked skin but with just a hint of the curve of her breast. She grabbed another towel from the rack and began to rub herself down, drying herself off. She held the towel across her chest as she dried one arm and then the other. She lifted one leg and propped her foot on the edge of the bath to rub that leg before swapping to the other.

'God, Ruby, that's not fair.' Noah's voice was a soft, deep groan.

'You're not the only one who likes a challenge,' she said, as she straightened up and wrapped the towel around her chest, tucking one end inside the other to hold it in place. 'We'll soon see who can keep up with whom, won't we?'

'I'm feeling better already,' he said, as he looked her up and down, and suddenly she wasn't sure that the towel offered enough protection against the force of his gaze.

'No, you're right. You need time to regain your strength. I don't want you falling apart on me. Besides, we haven't got all day,' she continued. 'I need to get you to your physio appointment.' Now that their intentions were clear Ruby knew there would be time later to act on their feelings. She just hoped she didn't have to wait too long.

Ruby and Noah spent the rest of that day and the next dancing around the issue of their attraction. She was being paid to take care of him and she was sure the rules would prevent her from having any sort of physical relationship with him. She wasn't having second thoughts about what she wanted, only about what was ethical. But it was a moot point really. He was still in a lot of pain, particularly by the end of the day, and she knew he wasn't ready for sex, despite what he thought.

Showering him in the morning was sweet torture—seeing him naked for all the wrong reasons was driving her crazy—but she wanted to make sure he could go the distance and she didn't want to risk any further injury.

Ruby had never been with anyone twenty-four seven before. Trying to do her job and ignore their chemistry was exhausting. And Noah wasn't the most compliant patient. He was finding it difficult being confined to a chair, and he was struggling with sitting still. Ruby suspected the problem was being compounded by sexual frustration but there was little she could do about that at the moment.

To pass the time and to distract them from their attraction they spent hours talking. They had a crash course in getting to know each other's likes and dislikes. Ruby loved green tea, strawberries and eggs Benedict. Noah loved coffee and mangoes and bacon but, like her, he didn't drink alcohol. His favourite music was Aussie rock, hers was pop and dance music. He liked to exercise first thing in the morning, loved surfing and paddle boarding but hated running. Ruby preferred to sleep in but she would get out of bed early for Noah—after all, he was paying her to—but she refused to exercise. She liked foreign movies, especially French ones, while he liked thrillers.

She could handle all those differences. They just made things more interesting. What she wasn't so sure about were the differences in their lifestyles. She was surprised at how lucrative motor racing was and how expensive Noah's tastes were. He didn't seem pretentious but he certainly liked the finer things in life. From his clothes to his groceries, everything was a brand name.

She guessed she wouldn't mind expensive things but she had never been able to afford them. Most of her clothes came from second-hand shops or the occasional chain store. She'd never had large amounts of money to spend on her wardrobe and she didn't see the point. She moved so frequently that it was easier to leave behind things she'd grown tired of—including boyfriends and clothes. She could always find another boyfriend and she could always find something to wear in the local charity shop. Noah, on the other hand, had expensive tastes—designer clothes, designer watches and designer sunglasses.

He did argue that a lot of his things, including his watch and sunglasses, were sponsors' products and therefore hadn't cost him anything. Ruby could see his point but she could also see that he had grown very used to having the best that money could buy—whether or not that money was his wasn't the point. But, at the end of the day, it wasn't her problem and she wasn't going to let it interfere with the next few weeks. She was determined to enjoy herself despite any differences.

Thursday, 25th December

'Merry Christmas.'

Ruby had got into the habit of waking Noah with a glass of orange juice and a handful of vitamins, and today was no exception. Mornings were almost his favourite time of the day. He was slow to get moving and needed a shower to warm up his muscles but that meant a chance to see Ruby semi-naked. After the first morning she'd taken to wearing a bikini when she showered him. He kept hoping for a repeat of her striptease but seeing her in a bikini was a reasonable alternative.

She stood in front of him wrapped in a thick, white, towelling dressing gown but he knew that underneath that she would be wearing nothing but her bikini. He could re-create that picture without any effort. He already knew her body intimately. But only by sight. He could close his eyes and picture every curve, every angle, every freckle. He knew her left eye tooth was slightly crooked, he knew the exact colour of her green eyes and that her second toes on both feet were longer than her first. He knew she preferred not to wear a bra and that her legs were long and pale and gorgeous. He knew her lips were soft and she tasted of strawberries but he was desperate to know more.

He wanted to taste the hollow at the base of her throat, to feel the softness of the skin on the inside of her thigh and to trace the curve of her hip. He was longing to know if the spot where her neck joined her shoulder also smelt like berries and how her body felt under his. How she would respond to his touch, how she would sound.

He knew there was a promise of things to come. The touch of her fingers as she dried his skin, the moments when her hands remained on his chest just a little longer than necessary or when he saw her watching him in the reflection of the bathroom mirror all told him that she wanted him as badly as he wanted her. He knew that these things would happen but he wasn't sure how much longer he could wait.

'Merry Christmas,' he answered, as he ran one hand over the roughness of his beard and sat up, carefully swinging his legs out of bed. He was consciously attempting to make these movements seem as painless and as easy as possible in the hope that Ruby would think he was healing faster than expected. He was eager to speed up the process, eager to get to the carrot at the end of the stick. Ruby was that carrot. He had two goals. One was to have Ruby, the other was to get back behind the wheel of his racing car, and each goal was as enticing as the other, although at the moment he'd be happy just to have Ruby in his bed.

He reached for the handful of tablets and washed them down with the orange juice as he glanced at the bedside clock. 'How much time do we have?'

'Two hours,' she replied, as she drew back the curtains. The sun was shining and all Noah could see was a flawless blue sky. It looked like a perfect summer's day. 'We have to be at Jake's parents' by ten.'

Ruby was smiling and he could see that some of the tension she'd been carrying in her shoulders had eased. He knew she was looking forward to today and he could understand why. She'd had a rough couple of weeks but he knew that today marked a turning point for her.

Rose was doing well and although she still wasn't fully recovered—and no one could tell them if and when that might happen—the doctors had considered her condition stable enough to allow her a leave pass from the hospital for a half day. With Rose's progress and the fact that Jake's five siblings and their partners were all gathered together for Christmas, Scarlett and Jake had decided that Christmas Day presented the perfect opportunity to get married.

The wedding would be a family affair at Jake's parents' home, followed by Christmas lunch, but when Scarlett had learned that Noah had no plans she'd insisted that Ruby bring him along too. He would be the only non-family member there but no one seemed to mind. Jake's family was large; one extra person would hardly be noticed.

'Do you think you'd have time to shave my beard this morning?' he asked. 'It's starting to get itchy and I look like a scruff but I can't shave left-handed.'

Ruby showered him and wrapped a towel around his waist and another around his bare shoulders in preparation for shaving his beard. She ran warm water into the basin and held the razor under it. She stood over his right shoulder and began with his left cheek.

She rested her fingers under his chin as she tilted his head towards her. The movement brought his eyes in line with her belly button and the soft swell of her stomach. She'd ditched the dressing gown when she'd showered him and hadn't put it back on. There were only three tiny triangles of bikini fabric between him and her bare flesh.

She drew the razor from his cheek down to his chin

before rinsing it and repeating the movement. Her fingers were soft on his skin and when they brushed over his lips he felt her touch light a fire that burned from his mouth to his belly and beyond. He bit back a moan. He didn't think he could stand much more of this. It was pleasure and pain rolled into one.

She tipped his head back to shave beneath his chin and jaw, bringing their heads close together and their lips even closer. He was just about to reach for her, unable to resist much longer, when she stood up and patted his face dry with a towel.

'God, Ruby, how much longer are you going to make me wait?'

'Until I'm sure you're up to it.' She grinned and he knew she'd choreographed all her movements very carefully to drive him to distraction.

It had worked. 'I'm up to it now, believe me.'

'Not much longer, I promise,' she said, bent over in front of him and picked the wet towels up from the bathroom floor. She glanced back at him over her shoulder, catching him staring at the spot where the strip of bikini fabric disappeared between her thighs. One tug on the string at the side of her hip and he could put them both out of their misery.

'Merry Christmas,' she added with a wink, as she straightened up.

The vision of her bending over before him would stay with him all day. Merry Christmas indeed.

The wedding service was brief. Scarlett and Jake really only needed the formalities and Noah paid no attention anyway. He only had eyes for Ruby. She had arrived at Jake's parents' in her usual casual clothes but somehow in the time between arriving and the service she'd been transformed, with the help of one of Jake's sisters, into something magnificent.

He was pleased he hadn't been able to travel for Christmas. Normally he would spend Christmas on the farm with his parents and his younger brother, Sam, but his injuries had made that impossible. Instead he got to spend Christmas with Ruby, an outcome he was more than happy with.

He had always thought she was striking, interesting—noticeable without being traditionally beautiful—but today she looked amazing. She was such a bundle of contrasts. Her slight frame and husky voice, her round, youthful face and her wide sensual mouth but in the pale green silk bridesmaid's dress that matched her eyes she was stunning and he couldn't take his eyes off her.

She was relaxed and happy with no sign of the tension that enveloped her at times—either due to Rose's illness or to her relationship with her mother—and her relaxed demeanour only helped to further enhance her appearance.

She had dyed her hair back to her natural strawberry blonde, colouring over the pink, and the colour was a much better foil for the dress and her skin tone. She looked ethereal, like a Celtic fairy, and he spent the rest of the day watching her. He was also trying to work out how to convince her that he had recovered enough to stop dancing around the issue of their attraction and take their relationship to the next level. He wanted to get her out of that dress and into his bed. He'd never gone home with a bridesmaid before.

Just when he thought he was going to have to admit defeat, Ruby materialised in front of him.

'It's time to go,' she told him.

He'd been challenging Jake's eight-year-old nephew to a video game and his arm was starting to complain. The game had become a little competitive and he'd probably overdone it but he wasn't about to admit that to Ruby. But she must have picked up on it somehow and had decided it was time to take him home. He wasn't about to argue. He was ready to have her undivided attention. As selfish as it seemed, he wasn't used to sharing her like he'd had to do today.

Ruby had noticed the discomfort gradually creeping up on Noah after lunch and had kept a close eye on him until she'd decided he'd had enough activity for one day. He hadn't argued when she'd deemed it time to leave, which had confirmed her suspicions that he had done enough. But it did amaze her that she was able to read him so well after just a few days.

'Are you tired? Do you need to rest?' she asked, when they were back in the penthouse. She could see the pain etched on his face but he wasn't giving in anymore.

He shook his head. 'No, I have something for you. A Christmas present. I want to give it to you now.'

Ruby sat on the couch and waited as Noah took himself off to his room and returned with a large box made of glossy white cardboard and tied with a red-and-white ribbon. He handed her the package. 'Merry Christmas.'

Ruby rested the box on her lap as she untied the ribbon and took off the lid. She unfolded a layer of tissue paper and lifted the gift out.

'It's the dress we saw in the shop window.' She stood and held the dress in front of her. 'It's absolutely gorgeous. How did you get it?'

'I called the shop and had it delivered while you were visiting Rose.'

'That was very sneaky.' She was touched that he'd gone to that trouble for her but she wondered why. 'What's it for?' she asked. She couldn't imagine where she would wear it, as gorgeous as it was.

'For this,' he said, handing her an envelope.

The envelope had been opened. Ruby pulled out an invitation and read it. 'We're invited to a party at the home of Ron and Trudy Townsend? As in the media mogul Ron Townsend?'

'He's the team boss.'

'Team boss?'

'He owns the team I drive for.'

'He *owns* a racing team?'

'Someone has to,' Noah said. 'It takes a lot of money to race on the V8 circuit. And Ron is a huge motorsport fan,' he told her, as if that explained it. 'Every year he hosts a New Year's Eve party and as part of our contract he expects his drivers to attend. Luckily he puts on a good show, it's a lot of fun. We'll be his guests for two nights.

'I can't go.'

'Why not? Have you got other plans?'

'No, it's not that.' They both knew her plans revolved around him at present. 'But I can just imagine the type of party and the type of people who will be there. I'll be completely out of my depth.'

'Everyone will love you and I'll be there with you. I promised to do something fun with you when I got out of hospital. This is it. Have you ever spent New Year's Eve in Sydney?'

She hadn't but that didn't matter. She shook her head.

'You'll enjoy it, I promise.'

Ruby was still shaking her head.

'Let me tell you how this works,' Noah said. 'When someone offers to send their private jet to pick you up and take you to an extravagant New Year's Eve party at a house on Sydney Harbour to watch the fireworks you say, "Thank you, that would be lovely."'

'A private plane?'

'Yep, and when someone gives you a gift you say, "Thank you, I know just the occasion to wear this beautiful dress."'

Ruby looked down at the dress that was now lying in its nest of tissue paper. It was superb but it just raised more concerns. 'Thank you, it is a stunning dress but what will I wear for the rest of the weekend?' She waved a hand over Noah's gift. 'If this is any indication of what people will be wearing, I have absolutely nothing suitable. I brought one small bag with me and minimal items of clothing.'

But Noah wasn't going to listen to her excuses. 'Borrow something of Scarlett's, go shopping with my credit card, I don't care. You can wear your bikini all weekend, I don't mind. In fact, I reckon I wouldn't mind that at all.' He grinned and Ruby's heart raced a little faster in her chest. 'But I need you there with me. I can't manage without you. Now, are you going to argue or are you going to try on your present?'

She couldn't resist. Even if she intended to extricate herself from going to the party and therefore had no good reason to keep the dress, it couldn't hurt to try it on. She had to wear it at least once. She picked up the box and took it to her room.

She swapped her bridesmaid's dress for Noah's present then turned hesitantly to look at her reflection in the full-length mirror. She preferred not to look at herself but even she had to admit that the dress was gorgeous and suited her perfectly.

The design was simple but elegant. Sequins embellished a black, figure-hugging strapless dress that ended a few inches above her knees. The sequins had been applied to give the illusion of curves and the length of the dress showed off her favourite body part, her legs. It was a straightforward design but the embellishment turned it into something special.

Her hair and make-up were still in place from the wedding but she tucked the slick, side ponytail into a bun at the nape of her neck, streamlining her silhouette. This dress needed a simpler hairstyle, one that didn't distract from the perfect cut and fit.

The inky black of the dress highlighted and complemented her fair skin but she thought it would look better if her hair was a couple of shades darker. A deep, russet red might be more striking than strawberry blond. More sophisticated. That was the look she was after. She'd have to redye her hair before New Year's Eve. She loved the dress, she'd never owned anything so amazing, and she didn't think she could bring herself to return it. Which meant she'd have to go to Sydney with Noah.

Oh, well, some sacrifices were worth it. She grinned as she checked her reflection again. She adored it. She thought she looked elegant, which wasn't a look she normally felt she could carry off, but this was a confidence-building dress. She slipped her feet into the silver heels she'd worn with her bridesmaid dress and returned to the living area to thank Noah properly for his extremely generous gift.

He had transferred himself out of his wheelchair and was sitting on the modular leather couch. Ruby crossed the room and twirled in front of him.

'You look incredible.'

She felt incredible. She smiled at him. 'I've been practising my "Thank you". Would you like to hear it?'

'I'm kind of busy enjoying the view right now.'

'Oh, I think you'll want to make time for this,' she said, as she stretched one hand behind her and reached for the zip. 'Thank you for my present, I know just the right occasion to wear this beautiful dress but unfortunately this moment isn't it.' She pulled the zip down and the dress fell to the floor, pooling around her feet. She stepped out of the dress and stood in front of him wearing nothing but silver heels and a pair of tiny lace knickers.

CHAPTER SEVEN

HIS EYES WERE wide as he ran his gaze along the length of her body and Ruby smiled at his reaction. She could feel the heat in his gaze and it warmed and reassured her.

'You're right, you were totally overdressed for the occasion,' he said, as he reached out for her with his left hand and cupped her bottom. The swell of her buttock fitted perfectly into his palm and the heat of his hand seared through the lace of her knickers. He ran his hand slowly down the back of her thigh to the sensitive skin behind her knee, sending an intense bolt of desire through her.

He looked up at her, his pupils dark in his blue eyes, his expression hungry. 'You feel fantastic.'

His fingers rested momentarily over the pulse at the back of her knee before he ran his hand back up her leg. She could feel moisture pooling between her thighs and her legs were weak. He clasped her hand, intertwining her fingers with his, and pulled her towards him, settling her in his lap. She sat astride his hips, relieved not to have to stand any longer but careful not to sit too heavily on his right thigh. But he seemed oblivious to her weight.

She dipped her head and pressed her lips to his. She wound her fingers through his hair as they deepened their kiss. She opened her mouth and their tongues met and tasted. She could feel his erection pressing against the inside of her thigh. She shifted her hips a fraction, rubbing against him. Noah moaned.

Noah let go of her hand and moved his hand to her breast. Her nipple peaked under his touch and it was her turn to moan. His fingers trailed down between her breasts and over her stomach as he dipped his head and took her breast in his mouth. Ruby closed her eyes and arched her back as his lips closed around her and she was swamped by waves of desire.

'Wait.' She wanted to go slowly but she knew she wouldn't be able to hold back and she still needed to get him out of his clothes. This moment wasn't just about her. It was about both of them.

She opened her eyes and undid his shirt, one button at a time. She slid the shirt from his body, working around the sling. She ran her fingers over his chest and over the ridges of his abdominal muscles. She was familiar with the feel of him, she'd been running her hands over him all week as she'd showered him, but this time was different. This time she was allowed to revel in the touch of his body under hers. This time she was allowed to take a minute or two to enjoy the feel of his muscles beneath her fingers. This time the outcome was going to be different.

She slid her fingers under the waistband of his shorts and flicked the button open before unzipping the fly. She stood up to remove his knee brace and he lifted his hips to enable her to take off his shorts. They'd become very co-ordinated and worked in unison to get him undressed, but for the past few days it had been to get him ready for the shower. Her hands were shaking now.

'Are you sure you want to do this?' he asked.

'Yes.'

'You're not nervous?'

Ruby shook her head. 'No. I'm excited. Impatient, aroused, but not nervous. I've been waiting for this moment,' she said, as she stood back to admire him. She'd seen him naked before but this time he was glorious. She reached out to touch him. His skin was warm and every inch of his body was hard and firm.

'By the way,' she said as she ran her fingers along his erection, 'I quit.'

'You what?'

'I'll stay on as your housekeeper but if we're going to do this, I can't be your nurse anymore. Okay?'

'You know I'd agree to anything you said at this point in time,' Noah said, as he rested his head back on the couch.

Ruby smiled as she increased her pressure around his shaft. 'Do you accept my resignation?'

'There's a condom in the pocket of my shorts.'

She took that as a yes. She stood and retrieved the foil packet, holding it between her lips as she started to take off her knickers.

'Let me do that.' Noah's voice was thick and deep.

He reached for the lace with his left hand and slid the flimsy fabric down to her knees. Ruby stepped out of her underwear and was about to kick off her heels but Noah stopped her.

'Leave them on,' he said. His voice was so deep and quiet she could barely make out his words.

She left her shoes on as she tore the condom packaging. She knelt over him as she rolled the condom onto his shaft. Her knees were spread wide as she straddled him and Noah's fingers slid inside her, into her wetness. His thumb found the sensitive nub at her centre and she almost climaxed under the touch of his hand.

But that wasn't what she wanted. Not today.

She pushed his hand out of the way, taking control.

She wanted him inside her. She'd been waiting for this moment and she wanted to feel him. She wanted him to fill her.

She lifted her hips and lowered herself over him, taking him deep inside her.

She wanted to be gentle and she tried to be careful. She tried to be mindful of all his broken bits—his elbow, his collarbone, his ribs and his leg—but it was hard to hold back. She'd wanted this for so long, they'd been dancing around this moment all week, and now that they'd started she couldn't make herself take it slowly. She couldn't wait. If she had to wait any longer she would explode.

Noah thrust up into her. If he was in pain he wasn't showing any signs of it. He wasn't holding back and Ruby matched his rhythm. She put her hands on the back of the couch. Supporting her own weight was her only concession to his injuries as she lifted and lowered her hips and rode him towards satisfaction.

The peak came quickly, crashing over her, and she felt Noah shudder beneath her, joining her in the moment of release.

It might have been hurried but it was no less satisfying. Fast or slow, it wouldn't have mattered.

They had plenty of time to try all sorts of different ways but Ruby thought it might be hard to beat their first time. In her opinion it had been close to perfect.

* * *

Over the next week they developed an easy routine. Ruby would make them breakfast then help Noah with his exercises and stretches, before taking him to his various appointments. He had a few sponsor engagements, mainly interviews, and he would schedule these for late morning, which gave him time for a sleep in the afternoon while she went to see Rose. When she got home she would climb into his bed and wake him in any number of imaginative ways and when they had finished making love he would tackle another exercise session.

Ruby had talked Noah out of hiring another nurse, having decided she was happy to still perform those duties but in an unpaid capacity. As a compromise she was being paid a very generous housekeeper's wage and it was an agreement that suited them both.

Their days were full and busy and Ruby was happy. She felt comfortable with Noah and for once she wasn't thinking about running away. They made love, they talked and he listened without judging, and Ruby could be herself.

She had seen Scarlett blossom under Jake's attention as she was free to be herself. Ruby had wanted that too, but she hadn't been sure if she liked herself enough to let someone else see the real her. But Noah seemed to like her so maybe she was worth something. Having his approval made her like herself a little bit more. But she didn't want to think of the power he seemed to hold over her. She hadn't resisted his job offer and she knew she wouldn't resist the chance now to get to know him even more intimately. That had been her objective all along. She'd just need to be careful. He had a knack of getting her to divulge personal information about herself and she couldn't imagine sharing her body and all her thoughts with someone. That was a recipe for disaster. In her mind that gave them the power and with that power came the possibility that they could hurt her.

New Year's Eve

'Ruby, the limo is here.'

Ruby shoved her floppy sunhat onto her head and grabbed her handbag and oversized sunglasses when Noah called to her. He was waiting in the hall. By the time Ruby got to him the chauffeur had already taken their bags, leaving them to follow when they were ready.

He put his hand on her arm, waylaying her before she could get into the lift. He pulled her down to him and kissed her.

'You look fantastic.' She was wearing her maxi-dress with flat sandals, and with the oversized glasses and large hat she looked like she'd stepped out of the nineteen seventies. She had dyed her hair a dark russet red that shone and would be a good contrast to the dress Noah had given her for Christmas. 'I remember this dress,' he said. 'It's the one you wore in the shower on that first morning here at the apartment.'

Ruby could remember how she'd flirted with him that morning with her striptease. How much had changed since then. She smiled to herself as she stepped into the lift, thinking about what she had in store for him today.

She almost had to pinch herself when the chauffeur delivered them to the waiting aircraft. She still couldn't believe that Ron Townsend had sent his private jet just to collect Noah for his New Year's Eve party.

The plane was sleek, white and much larger than she'd

expected, and her heart plummeted as she wondered how many people were going to be aboard with them.

'Is there anyone else coming with us?' she asked.

'Not that I know of,' he replied. 'Why?'

'I don't want to share.'

'You want exclusive access? You haven't even got on board yet and you've already developed a celebrity attitude,' he teased.

'No, it's not that. I just assumed we'd have the plane to ourselves.'

It took a bit of organisation to get Noah on board. The plane wasn't really geared for passengers in wheelchairs, but that was the only negative. Once they were inside the aircraft, and alone—to Ruby's relief—she had no complaints. The interior of the plane was beautifully appointed with soft leather seats the colour of caramel that swivelled and reclined and small wooden side tables made of oak. Two flat-screen televisions were fitted into the walls and under their feet was plush cream carpet. It was all very modern, sleek and expensive.

'I can see why people get accustomed to the rich-and-famous lifestyle,' she said, as they settled into their seats and Carmelo, the male flight attendant, served them sparkling mineral water in crystal glasses.

'Our flight time today will be approximately two and a half hours,' Carmelo told them in a smooth Italian accent. 'Lunch will be served on the flight but please enjoy some light refreshments while we prepare for take-off.' He left a platter of hors d'oeuvres for them and disappeared into the front of the plane.

Ruby stifled a giggle. 'Do you think his accent is real?'

Noah smiled. 'I have no idea but it all adds to the experience, doesn't it?'

Ruby agreed and decided to settle in and enjoy it. It was likely to be a once-in-a-lifetime event for her and she intended to make the most of it.

As Carmelo cleared the remains of their lunch away, Ruby checked the time and excused herself to use the bathroom. When she re-emerged Carmelo was still in the lounge. Her excitement dissipated and her face fell.

'What's the matter?' Noah asked when he saw her expression.

Ruby sat on the arm of his chair and whispered in his ear. 'I didn't expect to have Carmelo hovering over us the whole time. I was hoping for a new experience, if you know what I mean?' Ruby didn't want to know if Noah had ever joined the mile-high club, it was enough to know that she hadn't and she wanted to and she wanted to do it with him. 'I wore this dress especially.' She opened her handbag and showed Noah a pair of tiny undies that she'd just removed in the bathroom.

His eyes lit up and he grinned and Ruby knew he was up for it. 'Are you going commando?' he asked.

'Yep.'

He laughed and told her, 'I'll take care of it.'

Ruby didn't know what he did but in the next moment Carmelo was beside them. 'Will there be anything else, Mr Christiansen?'

'No, thank you, Carmelo.'

'Very well. Enjoy the flight,' he said, before he disappeared into the cockpit, drawing the curtain closed between the lounge and the galley on his way.

'Are you sure he's gone?' Ruby asked.

'Positive.'

'Finally, we're alone.'

Ruby lifted her dress above her knees and straddled him. She bent her knees, tucking her feet under her bottom and sandwiching her thighs between Noah's and the armrests of the chair. She leant over and pushed back the lever on the side of his seat, lifting the footrest and reclining the seat.

Noah grinned. 'I'm beginning to see the attraction in flying in a private jet.'

Ruby bent her head and kissed him squarely on his mouth. She didn't know how long they had and she didn't intend to waste a minute.

Noah's fingers grazed her nipple through the thin fabric of her dress. As usual she wasn't wearing a bra and her nipple peaked in response to his touch and she moaned and parted her lips and took his tongue into her mouth.

She could feel the pressure of Noah's hand on the outside of her thigh as he slid it under her dress, loosening it and untucking it from behind her knees. She shifted her weight, lifting her bottom slightly so Noah could slide his hand between her legs and over the naked flesh between her thighs. She felt his fingers slide inside her; she knew she was wet, and she arched her hips, pushing against his hand.

She loosened his belt and undid the fly on his shorts. She pushed his clothes out of the way as much as possible and freed his erection. There wasn't time to get properly undressed. It wasn't important. It wasn't necessary. They had spent many hours over the past week exploring each other and getting to know each other intimately. Ruby could close her eyes and re-create Noah perfectly in her mind. Whether they'd been making love on the couch, in bed, on the daybed on the balcony or even on the baby grand piano, the sex had been fantastic. Sometimes urgent, sometimes slow but always satisfying.

His shaft was thick and warm in her palm and she could feel his pulse beating under her fingers.

His fingers were still inside her and his thumb was making little circles against her swollen clitoris. Ruby could feel her limbs starting to liquefy. She pushed her hips forward again, pushing herself against his thumb.

For Ruby today wasn't about taking it slow, it was all about the location and the experience.

But Noah had other ideas. 'Not yet,' he said. 'I don't have a condom.'

Her purse was lying on the seat beside them. She'd packed a condom in there deliberately. She emptied her purse and found the packet. She tore it open.

Noah withdrew his finger and watched her roll the condom onto his shaft. He lifted her hips and Ruby had to follow his lead, he wasn't able to lift her fully as he still only had one good arm to work with. He brought her down onto him, filling her, and Ruby breathed out as she took him inside her. Her breath came out in a sigh.

Noah moaned as he thrust into her and lifted her up and down.

Her breaths were coming faster now. She was breathing in time with his thrusts. There was no more sighing; she was getting progressively louder.

She arched her back as she took Noah into her time and time again.

Deeper. Harder. Faster.

Ruby could feel the waves of pleasure roll over her and she cried out as the orgasm swept her away. Noah shuddered as he came inside her and Ruby collapsed against his chest.

Her legs were like jelly. She couldn't feel her toes but she could feel her heart. It was racing so fast she could feel the blood pumping into her fingers. She loved this time with Noah—the afterwards—loved it almost as much as the sex. For a few minutes every day she could relax and just be. For a few minutes she could forget about everything else that was going on in her life.

Noah provided her with an escape, a very pleasant and satisfying escape.

While she rested against Noah the plane hit an air pocket and jolted her, bringing her attention back to her surroundings. She had forgotten all about Carmelo; she hadn't given a thought to how much noise she had made. She looked around, hoping he hadn't materialised unexpectedly.

'How noisy were we?' she asked Noah. 'You don't think Carmelo heard us, do you?'

'I wouldn't worry. Carmelo and the pilot would both have had headphones on.'

'Really?'

'Trust me.'

'I don't want to know how you know that.'

'They're very well trained,' Noah replied, with a laugh that made Ruby blush.

Thinking about Carmelo made her nervous about being caught in a compromising position. 'Do I need to make you decent?' She wasn't ready to move yet, she actually didn't think she could. She could feel Noah's heart beating under hers. It was a nice feeling.

'There's no hurry,' Noah said.

'What if Carmelo comes back?'

'He won't come out until I tell him we're ready.'

'And how do you do that?'

'I'll push the call button and then he'll know we're finished.'

'Oh, God,' Ruby said, as she buried her face in Noah's shoulder. 'He's going to know I'm a shameless wench.'

'Is there any other sort of wench?' he teased her. 'It's too late to be worrying about that now, don't you think?'

'Three, two, one! Happy New Year.'

The band began to play 'Auld Lang Syne' as fireworks exploded over Sydney Harbour. The display from the Harbour Bridge, the Opera House and from several barges moored on the water was magnificent but Ruby only had eyes for Noah.

In a room full of beautiful people he was by far the most handsome. His tuxedo fitted him like a glove, and so it should, having been made for him by one of his sponsors, a designer menswear label, and Ruby could see why they'd picked him. He wore a suit well. Until tonight she had only seen him in casual clothes—shorts and shirts—as they were the easiest things to get on over his sling and with the knee brace. She'd had to help him with his shirt buttons, his belt and his bow-tie. Tying his tie had almost made them late. Not because she couldn't do it but because it was such an intimate task and she'd been sidetracked by his proximity, they both had. But eventually they had both dressed and had made it to the party.

Ruby had been determined to have a night to remember. She doubted she'd ever have another chance to celebrate the start of a new year in a mansion overlooking one of the most spectacular harbours in the world, but she had made sure she was by Noah's side as the count-down had begun. She was going to make sure she was the one and only person he kissed when the clock struck midnight.

And when he kissed her she didn't care who saw them. She was happy for people to see they were to-gether. Being with Noah gave her confidence she lacked. He'd seemed to genuinely enjoy introducing her to his friends and colleagues and having his attention was be-ginning to make her believe she was worthy of being loved.

'Happy New Year. Have you had fun?'

'I have.'

The party had been great fun. She had danced and met some interesting people but the best thing about the night was the fact that she was Noah's date. She'd been aware of the admiring looks from several of the male guests when she had accompanied Noah into the party and she'd loved the look of pride she'd seen in his eyes when he'd noticed it too. She hadn't cared about the other men but knowing that Noah thought she looked fabu-lous had been worth a thousand appreciative glances from strangers.

'I liked watching you dance.'

'You did?'

He nodded. 'You dance the same way you make love. As if you really enjoy it.'

'They *are* my two favourite activities.' Ruby laughed as Noah reached for her with his left hand. He cupped her bottom and pulled her in against him and kissed her again.

'In that case, are you ready for bed?'

Noah had insisted on being out of his wheelchair for

the evening. He had propped himself on a bar stool and hadn't moved as the other guests had sought him out, but Ruby realised he was probably exhausted and needed to sit down properly.

'If you're coming with me, I am.'

Ruby lay curled against Noah's side, sated and happy but not at all tired. Even though they'd had a busy day, her mind was buzzing.

'Have you made a New Year's resolution?' she asked him.

'Not a New Year's one specifically. Just the same as before—to get back behind the wheel in time for the start of the season.'

'I heard you mention that to a few of the sponsors tonight. What will they say if you don't make it?'

'I'm going to make it. There's no prize for second best, as they say,' he said, reminding her how focussed and determined he was. 'What's your resolution?'

Ruby made the same one every year—to stay sober for another twelve months—but she wasn't ready to talk to Noah about that. She was sharing enough of herself already. 'I'm going to try to spend a bit more time in Adelaide.'

'You move a lot, don't you?' His voice was deep and soft. It vibrated in his chest and rumbled through her. She could lie in the dark and listen to him all night.

'I guess so, compared to other people maybe.'

'Why?'

'I'm not sure. I'm looking for somewhere that fits me and I haven't found it yet. Then I get itchy feet and have to move.' She didn't admit that her feet usually started itching when people started getting to know her. If people got too close it could hurt her when they left so she preferred to leave first, before she could form strong attachments. 'I thought I might fit better there now that I'm ten years older and maybe wiser. I might even be able to get on better with Mum.'

'Are you closer to your father?'

'No. I don't have any sort of relationship with him. I don't have anything to do with him and he doesn't have anything to do with me.'

'What about with your sisters? He wasn't at Scarlett's wedding.'

Ruby could hear the frown in Noah's voice. This was why she avoided talking about her family. It was complicated and painful.

'That's because he isn't Scarlett's father. We're half-sisters.'

'Half-sisters? Why haven't you told me this before?'

'Is it important?' Ruby was nervous about telling him more. What if it changed how he saw her? Even though the logical part of her brain told her that her mother's choices had nothing to do with her, she knew those choices had affected how she was raised and she didn't want them to alter Noah's perceptions of her. 'Does it change anything?'

'No, but it might help me to understand you.'

'I doubt it. It's complicated. *I'm* complicated.'

'I prefer to call you interesting.'

'Really?'

'Really. So why wasn't Scarlett's father at her wedding?'

Ruby had opened Pandora's box now and she could tell Noah wasn't going to be fobbed off easily. She debated about distracting him, she found sex was a pretty good distraction, but she suspected it wasn't going to work on him tonight.

'Scarlett has never met her father and mine ran off when I was a baby. Rose's father...'

'Rose's father?'

'Yep, we're all half sisters. I warned you it was complicated.' *In for a penny, in for a pound,* she thought. She might as well tell him the truth about her parentage, that wasn't exactly a secret. 'Rose's father married Mum when I was four. We are all Andersons because he adopted Scarlett and me and he was the closest thing I've had to a real dad, but he died when I was thirteen.'

'Did you ever see your father?'

'For a little while when I was a teenager. I had nothing to do with him until after Rose's dad died. I didn't know anything about him until then, I'd never asked any questions and Mum had never volunteered anything. When I was sixteen Mum and I went through a difficult period and I ran off to Melbourne to live with my father.'

'That's where you went when you left Adelaide? You ran away from home at sixteen?'

'Mum knew where I was going. She tried to talk me out of it but I wouldn't listen. I thought I knew best. It turns out I didn't know anything. My father didn't want me there, I just made his life complicated, so he ignored me. I guess Mum knew what she was talking about after all. She made some bad choices in her time and he was one of them.'

'What happened between them?'

'He and Mum met when she worked in a nursing home and he was a rep for a medical-supply company— he was your typical travelling salesman. They had what Mum thought was a serious relationship but he neglected to tell her that he was already married *and* had a family who lived in Melbourne. That little bit of information didn't come out until Mum fell pregnant with me. That obviously wasn't part of his plan and he panicked and took off, back to his first family, leaving Mum with Scarlett and me. Mum had Scarlett when she was just eighteen. Scarlett's father never knew about her, it was Mum's decision to keep the baby against the father's family's wishes, so suddenly she found herself a single mother twice over.'

'So what happened when you went to Melbourne?'

'Dad was going through a divorce and I think having me there was like rubbing salt into the wound. I'm positive Mum wouldn't have been the only woman he'd had an affair with but she might have been the first one he had to admit to and I think he blamed me in a way. If Mum hadn't got pregnant with me, he might have got away with his infidelities. He didn't really want anything to do with me and I didn't like being there all that much either, but I'd made my bed when I'd run away from home and I refused to admit my mistake. I couldn't go back, not immediately, so I stuck it out in Melbourne and just made matters worse.'

Telling him about her parentage was one thing; confiding her complete family history was another thing altogether, and it was something she normally didn't share. There was too much that could hurt her.

It was one reason she kept her relationships short. If it was casual she wouldn't be expected to divulge her deepest, darkest secrets and thoughts. But she had surprised herself with the things she'd shared with Noah but she knew it was because she had a sense that he wouldn't hurt her. She hoped she was right.

'He blamed his estranged teenage daughter for his failings as a husband and father?' Noah asked. 'Didn't he take ownership of his mistakes?'

'Not really. I think he just moved on, leaving his messes behind.'

For the first time Ruby wondered if she had more of her father's traits in her than she'd realised. Did her tendency to run come from him? Was she less like her mother than she'd thought? Lucy was a fighter. She had fought to keep her children and Ruby was horrified to think that she might take after her father after all.

'I'm sorry, Ruby,' Noah said, as he hugged her a little closer. 'Everyone deserves to have parents who love them unconditionally.'

It was a good feeling to know that Noah had her back. Ruby had always depended on Scarlett for that but it would be nice to have more than one person in her corner. Lying in the dark tucked against Noah's chest with his arm around her, she felt as if nothing could hurt her. She felt as though this was where she belonged. Maybe the place she'd been searching for was beside Noah.

But was that a dangerous thought? Was she setting herself up for disappointment? The answer was probably yes but now that the thought had entered her head she found it hard to shift.

She put it to one side, choosing the path of least resistance. She'd deal with it later. For now she was going to enjoy the moment.

CHAPTER EIGHT

Wednesday, 11th February

JANUARY HAD FLOWN past and February seemed to be in just as much of a hurry. Noah's rehab had progressed well and Ruby was amazed at the speed of his recovery but, until today, she'd been successfully ignoring the fact that every step that he took towards a full recovery was taking him one more step away from needing her.

He had ditched his sling and the wheelchair and was now mobile on a pair of crutches. His big physical assessment was two days away and he was positive that he was on track to be back behind the wheel after that.

Ruby had been crossing the days off one by one on the makeshift calendar on the penthouse window. She was well aware of the date and of the fact that she'd known Noah for almost nine weeks.

Nine weeks. She'd let herself stay far longer than she'd intended to. Her relationships *never* lasted this long.

She tried to convince herself that this time was different, this time it was her job. Noah was paying her to be his housekeeper but she was free to walk away at any time.

But she knew that wasn't true.

The longevity had nothing to do with her employment and everything to do with their physical and emotional relationship. And that was the problem. Physical relationships she could handle but emotional relationships were a different matter altogether.

Ruby had become very comfortable with Noah and over the past weeks she'd gradually revealed more and more of her true self. She had never wanted to do that before and she hadn't really intended on sharing quite so much with Noah, but when they talked he listened and she found herself telling him things she would normally never reveal. She had worried that he'd judge her but that wasn't the case. He was allowing her to be herself and, even better, he seemed to like the real her. She had never been sure if she liked herself but knowing that Noah liked her made her feel as if she was worth something.

As the weeks passed Ruby had a growing sense that she belonged with Noah. This might not have been a problem except for the fact that she suspected her feelings for him ran deeper than his for her, and that wasn't something she was used to. Her relationships normally served a purpose—mutual satisfaction—and nothing more. Normally she could take or leave a partner; normally anyone could alleviate her loneliness. But Noah was different. She feared she had grown to need him but she suspected his need for her wasn't as compelling.

Was she just a convenience?

But despite these misgivings she couldn't make herself walk away. She enjoyed his company and she enjoyed sharing his bed. Even if he only needed her for convenience, that was enough. She'd worry about the implications of this relationship once he no longer needed her at all.

She dumped the shopping bags onto the kitchen counter. She'd been to the supermarket to buy the ingredients for the celebratory dinner she was planning. Tomorrow they were flying to Sydney for his physical test, which was scheduled for Friday—Friday the thirteenth. She hoped that wasn't a bad omen. If he passed he'd be allowed back behind the wheel for the test runs on Saturday the fourteenth. That was the date he'd been aiming for since day one. The big day was almost here.

Ruby knew she shouldn't be planning on celebrating tonight—he hadn't passed yet—but she was convinced he would. In her eyes he certainly seemed to have made a full recovery but his recovery was a double-edged sword. If Noah was allowed to drive, he wouldn't need her anymore.

She began unpacking the groceries, surprised he hadn't come to help her. Since he'd achieved the milestones he'd set himself and had become mobile, he was almost always on hand to help her. There wasn't much he couldn't do for himself now, except drive.

She went looking for him, there weren't too many places he could be, and found him on the balcony. There was a bottle of spirits on the table in front of him. Along with one glass. The bottle was open. She could smell the alcohol. She recognised the scent—rum.

Ruby frowned.

Why was he drinking? And especially why was he drinking when the driving test was imminent? He'd told her he didn't drink. He'd told her it didn't fit with his job description. She'd believed him, she'd had no reason not to, and she hadn't seen anything to contradict his words. Until now.

She stepped out onto the balcony. 'What are you doing?'

'Making a toast.'

'But you don't drink.' She didn't mention the obvious—that he was alone and it was kind of difficult to make a toast when you were the only one in the room.

'It's been ten years,' he said.

'I don't understand.' Who would choose to celebrate ten years of soberness by opening a bottle of rum?

He looked up at her and Ruby was shocked by the dullness of his eyes. It was more than alcohol, he looked exhausted. She'd never seen him look so defeated, not even in the early days when he'd been in significant pain. 'I'm drinking a toast to my brother. Grab a glass and join me.'

She remembered he had mentioned a brother who lived on the family farm. Sam. Something had obviously happened but it didn't look as though it was something Noah was happy about. So why a toast? She had no idea what he was talking about.

She chose to ignore his invitation to fetch a glass and instead pulled out a chair at the table and turned it to face him before sitting down. 'Your brother? Sam? Why?' Had he had bad news? No, bad news wouldn't warrant a toast.

'No. Adam.' Noah's eyes were dark, and all traces of the brilliant blue sparkle she'd grown to love had been erased. 'He died ten years ago today. This is the one day of the year when I have a drink. A toast to his memory.'

Ruby glanced at the bottle. It seemed to her that he

was doing more than toasting his brother's memory. He was halfway to obliterating it *and* the bottle.

She didn't really want to sit there and watch him drink. She always did her best to steer clear of temptation and avoided situations that revolved purely around drinking. But luckily rum had never been her choice of poison and she knew he needed her there. She could sit with him and perhaps if she got him talking about his brother he'd slow down on the rum. She'd only been at the shops for a short time, a little over an hour, but he'd made a serious dent in the level of the bottle. It was already half-empty.

Someone else might argue that it was half-full but Ruby had always seen a bottle of alcohol as half-empty and therefore it might as well be finished.

Where had it come from? She knew what was in the cupboards, she'd been doing all the shopping. He must have had it delivered, she realised. He'd organised other deliveries, her Christmas present included, but this wasn't such a nice surprise. Looking at the slightly glazed expression in his blue eyes and listening to the slight blurriness of his deep voice, she knew it had been full when he'd started so it must have been new. Had he deliberately waited until she'd gone before he'd opened it?

And why had he kept the significance of today a secret? Why hadn't he said anything to her?

Those questions just confirmed for her that her feelings towards him weren't reciprocated in the same way. She needed to start thinking about leaving. She needed to look for her own replacement or hope he passed the driving test tomorrow. Then she could be on her way. But she would not walk out on him tonight. She wouldn't leave him to drown his sorrows alone. The least she could do was sit with him and listen if he wanted to talk, even if she wouldn't join him in a drink.

She hadn't had to make excuses to him for her own abstinence. He had never asked for more explanation than she'd originally given and she'd never volunteered any details about her vow of sobriety—that would have been divulging too much of herself. Giving him her body was easier than giving him her history. She hadn't wanted him to judge her so she wouldn't judge him now. How he chose to mourn or remember his brother was his business.

'How old was he?'

'Eighteen.'

Ruby knew that Noah was four years older than his brother, Sam. Ten years ago Noah would have been twenty so Adam would have also been younger than him. The middle brother.

Noah didn't seem to mind answering her question. He was obviously aware of her presence, not too caught up in his reminiscing, so she felt comfortable asking the next question. 'What happened?'

He swirled the rum around in his glass and the aroma made Ruby feel queasy. 'He'd been out in one of the paddocks, repairing a fence. He was a long way from the house.' Ruby wondered what distance had to do with anything but she didn't want to interrupt. 'I was on the other side of the farm, repairing a windmill,' he continued. 'When he wasn't home in time for dinner I said I'd go and look for him. It was a hot day and I thought maybe he hadn't been able to work as quickly as he wanted to. I thought I'd give him a hand to finish off. I didn't want to think that he might have had an accident.

All sorts of things can go wrong on a farm but nine out of ten times when people are late it's nothing. Just normal delay...'

Noah's voice trailed off as he remembered. Ruby waited, wondering if he was going to finish or if the memories were too painful.

'I found him.' His voice caught on the words. 'He was in his ute. The driver's door was open and I could see his feet sticking out. I thought he'd fallen asleep but when I got closer I saw the blood. His blood.' Noah rubbed his hand over his face. 'Splattered across the windscreen. Blood and brains and bits of bone.'

'He'd been killed?'

Noah shook his head. 'He killed himself.'

'Oh, Noah, I'm so sorry.' Ruby reached out and put her hand over his, connecting her to him. She had counselled teenagers before who had lost friends to suicide but it was so much harder when she was emotionally invested. She didn't know what else to say.

'In one hand was his rifle, we always carried a rifle with us, we never knew when we might have to put a sheep down. In his other hand was a letter. I thought maybe it was a suicide note but it wasn't. It was a letter from his girlfriend. Telling him she was moving to Sydney. She didn't want to live in the country. She was sorry but she couldn't imagine spending the rest of her life out in the middle of nowhere.

'That was all Adam wanted. To be a farmer. And I know they'd talked about getting married, even though they were young they had plans, he had plans and he'd wanted to make a life with her on the farm. The property was profitable and I was pleased one of us wanted to take it on. It meant I was free to pursue my dream.

But Annabel crushed Adam's dream so badly that he hadn't been able to see any other future.

'The letter was dated a month earlier. He hadn't said anything to any of us. He hadn't asked for help. He'd kept it all bottled up. None of us had any idea. And we hadn't been with him at the end. There was only Jessie.'

'Jessie?'

Noah hadn't touched his drink since she'd sat down with him but he was making less and less sense.

'His sheepdog.'

'Was she alive?'

'Yes. Adam would never hurt Jessie and she was always by his side. She wouldn't leave him.'

Now Noah's earlier comment about how far from the house Adam had been made sense. Ruby knew that Noah thought if Adam had been closer to the house maybe the dog would have come running back. Ruby knew it would have still been unlikely that they would have been able to save him but at least they might have known sooner what had happened and maybe had less guilt.

'It was almost more than Dad or I could bear when he had to put Jessie down too.'

'What had happened to her?'

'She was dying of a broken heart. The same as Adam. She refused to eat, she was wasting away. Dad had no choice but it was almost more than any of us could stand. And after that Dad and I drowned our sorrows. Night after night. And if I wasn't drinking with Dad I was drinking with my mates. I'd been offered a chance to drive with a racing team, I'd been given my big break, but I nearly blew it. My mother read me the Riot Act— she didn't want to lose two sons and if I insisted on drinking and driving fast cars there was a good chance she would lose me too.

'I decided I wanted to pursue the chance I'd been given. Killing myself wasn't going to bring Adam back so I decided to give up the booze and now I just drink a toast to him once a year.' He picked up his glass and asked, 'So, are you going to get a glass and join me?'

She could see the shadows in his blue eyes. Had he forgotten she didn't drink? Or didn't he care? Had the memories and the grief and the rum wiped everything else from his mind?

Ruby's hand shook as she reached for the bottle.

She didn't want to be rude or to ignore his brother's memory but she couldn't do it. It might be ten years since Noah had lost his brother but it was also ten years since she'd last had a drink and she wasn't going to break a decade of sobriety. Not for anyone. Not even Noah.

'I think you've had enough for both of us,' she said as she picked up the bottle and the lid and started to screw the cap on.

Noah's hand shot out and covered hers. The rum didn't appear to have dulled his reflexes.

'I'm a big boy. I can look after myself.'

Ruby had no intention of sitting there while he proceeded to finish off the contents of the bottle, and she suspected that was his plan. Surely that could kill a man.

'I'll make you a coffee and bring you a jug of water but I'm not going to join you. Drinking doesn't solve anything. It only makes things worse.'

'That's right. I almost forgot—you don't drink.' Noah looked at her properly for the first time since she'd walked onto the balcony. 'When are you going to tell me what that's all about?'

'When I think it's important for you to know,' she said. She doubted he'd remember anything they talked about in the morning but she wasn't willing to take that chance. Some things were better left unsaid.

'You know, you're an enigma. It's all very well to be mysterious but there comes a time in a relationship when you need to open up. That's what relationships are about.'

And that was what frightened her. She'd known this moment would come, it always did, which was why she usually had a self-imposed two-month time limit on re-lationships. She knew he would expect her to share at some point. But she couldn't do it. She wasn't ready to tell him why she didn't drink. Guilt and pain and sor-row made her go on the attack.

'That works both ways. Not once have you mentioned the significance of today to me. You've never mentioned Adam. The first time I hear about him is when I find you demolishing a bottle of rum and ruining your chances for the weekend. I don't think you get to lecture me about sharing.'

She stood up. 'I think you should get some sleep. We're flying to Sydney tomorrow. You've got your phys-ical assessment and your simulator test in two days. You've done all the hard work at rehab. Don't let the past nine weeks be for nothing. You need to remember how much you wanted this chance all those years ago. Don't blow it now. Tomorrow is your only chance to get cleared to get back in a race car in time for round one of the championship. Ask yourself how badly do you want it? Do you want it more than you want that next drink?'

CHAPTER NINE

Thursday, 12th February

NOAH FELT AS if something had crawled into his mouth in the night and sucked all the moisture out of him. His head was pounding. He rolled over and groaned as his head threatened to explode and the events of the previous night gradually filtered through his foggy brain. The expression on Ruby's face was one of the first things that came to mind. Disappointment had been etched over it. She'd left him on the balcony but not before she'd lectured him on the error of his ways.

He had to admit she had a point. And he'd listened. He'd left the cap on the bottle and drunk the water and ignored the coffee, knowing it would only dehydrate him more, but he hadn't expected to feel quite so average this morning.

He was alone in his bed. He knew Ruby hadn't slept there last night. The pillow beside his had no indentation in it and her scent was absent. It seemed as though she'd kept her distance. He'd have to apologise for his behaviour. He suspected he'd been fairly antisocial.

He sat up gingerly, pleased to find the room wasn't spinning and his stomach wasn't heaving. He stood.

His leg was stiff but that was nothing new. After a hot shower and the stretches that had become part of his morning routine he knew most of the stiffness would abate. He checked the time. He needed to get into the shower. He needed as much time as possible to get his leg moving. It had to be better. His future depended on it. He had to prove he'd recovered enough to get back behind the wheel of a V8 racing car.

He couldn't believe he'd let his emotions get the better of him last night. What had he been thinking? The alcohol had knocked him around more than usual—he knew it was because he wasn't fully fit or fully recovered—but he'd hoped he was recovered enough to get through his physical. He couldn't believe he'd jeopardised his chances like that last night. Fortunately for him, Ruby had been there to talk some sense into him.

Snippets of their conversation slowly filtered into his consciousness. He had a suspicion he'd offered her a drink. He couldn't believe he'd done that. He knew she didn't drink—he didn't know why and he remembered now she'd refused to tell him, but he should never have offered her one. He knew he wouldn't have if he'd been even semi-sober. No wonder she'd avoided his bed. He'd been rude and unpleasant and he was mortified that he'd treated her that way. He needed to find her and apologise for his behaviour.

Ruby was in his room when he came out of the bathroom. She was dressed but she avoided eye contact. She handed him some paracetamol tablets and a glass of water and got ready to help him with his stretches, as she did every morning, but there was no accompanying banter, no smile, nothing. She was all business, no pleasure.

'I owe you an apology,' he said, as she stretched his

calf. 'I think I offered you a drink. I'm sorry, I shouldn't have done that.'

'It doesn't matter. I make my own decisions.'

Her reply was short and sharp. She was obviously annoyed at him and he suspected she had good reason to be.

'I'm still sorry. I don't normally have such bad manners. I was poor company last night but I did listen to your suggestion and I did go to bed so I want to thank you for your cool head and wise words.'

'It's up to you how you choose to remember your brother but I hope you haven't screwed up your chances for your test tomorrow.'

Ruby noticed that he didn't apologise for his drinking, which was good, she didn't feel he owed her an apology for that. His drinking wasn't the issue. She did feel like he had let her down but she was the one who had put him on the pedestal. She'd thought he was perfect and she should have known better. No one was perfect. She realised her expectations of him had been unreasonable and it wasn't her place to judge him now. She was far from perfect herself.

But she was annoyed that he'd offered her a drink and she was annoyed that he hadn't told her about his brother. But she did have the good grace to realise she was being unfair. Although she had shared many personal stories with him, there were plenty more she had kept to herself, including the real reason why she didn't drink, and it was hypocritical of her to expect one kind of behaviour from him when she wasn't prepared to do the same.

But she did wonder why he hadn't shared the significance of the day with her until he'd been halfway to being drunk. Obviously the sharing wasn't an issue but the timing was, and Ruby felt it confirmed what she'd suspected—that his feelings towards her weren't as strong as hers were towards him.

She knew he was focused on achieving his goal of being cleared to drive by February fourteenth, but she couldn't believe he hadn't once mentioned the significance of the twelfth. He couldn't have forgotten about it, the dates were too close together for it to have slipped his mind, and judging by his behaviour last night there was no way he had forgotten, which meant he'd deliberately chosen not to tell her. He'd deliberately chosen to shut her out.

It was definitely time to start thinking about her exit strategy.

It had been nine weeks.

Nine weeks that they'd known each other, almost eight weeks that they'd been living together and seven that they'd been sleeping together. She'd got too involved too quickly, even by her standards.

It was time to go.

Friday, 13th February

It had been a tense twenty-four hours. The events of Wednesday night shadowed their movements and eavesdropped on their conversation and Ruby was well aware that she was more short-tempered and feistier than normal and it was almost with a sense of relief that she dropped Noah off for his battery of tests.

He was going to spend a full day undergoing a range of assessments—reflex testing, mobility tests, strength, fitness and then into the simulator. There was no need for her to go with him, it would do her good to have some space and time to work out how she was feeling.

She had her day all mapped out. She was going to wander through the Rocks and take a ferry trip and find a market or two to browse. But her day didn't go according to plan.

Ruby was lonely.

She was used to being lonely, she didn't particularly like it but she was usually able to entertain herself, but she missed Noah. It was the longest they had spent apart in eight weeks. She told herself she would adjust, it wasn't as if they were going to be together for ever but it was the first time she'd ever missed a person.

She thought she'd always been wandering, looking for a place to belong, but perhaps it might not be a place she'd been searching for. Perhaps it was a person.

She was constantly thinking, *I wish Noah was here to see this,* or wanting to talk to him, but he wasn't there. They had spent so much time together over the past two months that it was going to take some adjusting to being without him, but she knew that soon, maybe even as soon as today, he wouldn't need her anymore.

She did some shopping at the Bondi markets. She bought a couple of things for herself and a T-shirt for Noah but when she got back to the hotel and saw all his designer clothes hanging in the wardrobe she realised he would never wear what she'd just bought him. It wasn't his style. It was just another reminder of how different they really were.

Ruby didn't need Noah to tell her the results of his test. She could see on his face that he'd passed. He was grinning from ear to ear when she arrived to collect him.

He wrapped his arms around her waist and picked her up and spun her around, as excited as a child. 'We did it!

'You passed.'

Ruby wasn't quite as excited as he was but his exuberance was infectious and it was hard not to be happy for him. She *was* happy for him, of course she was.

Noah took her out to celebrate and she tried to have a good time. She used to be so good at pretending to have fun. She needed to remember how to do that.

'What time do you need to be at the track for testing tomorrow?' she asked. Tomorrow was the testing day for the cars. Another day of wandering around, waiting for Noah, loomed in front of her.

'Eight o'clock. I'm not driving tomorrow, the team don't want to risk it, but I'll be out there, watching. You're welcome to come with me.'

She didn't want to spend the day sitting around, waiting for him. That wasn't where she wanted this relationship to go.

'And then I thought we could go and visit my parents,' he added. 'They're only a three-hour drive from here.'

Ruby had two options. She could go with him or she could leave. Both options frightened her.

If she went with him it would mean moving their relationship onto another stage. She didn't want to meet his parents. In her eyes that was taking a step deeper into the relationship when she should be extricating herself. A more committed stage would mean he would expect more from her and he already knew more about her than anyone else did. All that was left to tell him was what had really happened when she'd run away to Melbourne and she didn't think she could do that. Which only left the alternative—not having him in her life at all. And she knew, from the past twenty-four hours, how that felt and she hadn't liked it.

But when she got scared she had two choices. Fight or flight.

And she always chose flight.

'I'm not a "meet-the-parents" type,' she told him.

'What does that mean?'

'It's not my thing.'

'What? You've never met any of your boyfriends' parents?'

'Nope. Why would I need to?'

'Oh, I don't know. Maybe because that's what people do when they're in a relationship. They get to know the other important people in each other's lives.'

'We've been in a relationship for five minutes. It's not as if it's serious.'

'Isn't it?'

He sounded cross. She'd never heard him cross before and she didn't like it. She didn't want him to be cross, she wanted him to tell her how he felt. But of course he didn't.

'Why won't you let me close? You have put up so many barriers that whenever I get past one it's only to find another one in my way. What are you afraid of?'

'Nothing,' she lied.

'Is this like Ron's New Year's Eve party? Are you worried about people judging you? My parents aren't like that, they will love you.'

But she was pretty sure his parents wouldn't be expecting someone like her. They'd only need one look at her to see how different she was from their son. She'd grown up in a single-parent house with no money. He had everything he could possibly want. They really didn't have anything in common.

'I've met your family,' he said. 'Can't you do the same for me?'

She couldn't. She didn't know what she'd do instead but she had all day tomorrow to figure it out.

Saturday, 21st February

Scarlett's daughter lay in Ruby's lap, looking up at her with her dark eyes. At one week of age Holly was the image of her mother and had totally captured Ruby's heart. Captured all of them. The whole family was enamoured of this tiny doll of a child.

She had left Noah in Sydney one week ago when Scarlett had gone into labour and given her the perfect excuse to flee. She had left him to visit his parents alone but she couldn't stop thinking about him.

They'd had their second argument in less than a week and she knew it was her fear that was heightening the tension between them and making her disagreeable. She was so afraid that he wouldn't want her that she was pushing him away. She knew she was doing it but she seemed powerless to stop herself. Just like she couldn't stop thinking about him.

Noah had offered her the use of the penthouse as it was being rented for the team until after the opening race of the season but Ruby couldn't bear to stay there without him. She had loved the penthouse before but returning to it now she realised that what she'd loved about it was that it had felt like their own private hideaway from the world and it wasn't the same without Noah in it. Nothing was the same without Noah. But she'd have to learn to live like that.

Scarlett had lost a lot of blood during the delivery and the baby wasn't feeding all that well so Ruby had moved in with Scarlett and Jake to lend a hand. It was good to be busy and she was finding Holly to be a useful distraction from her almost constant thoughts of Noah.

Ruby and Lucy were supposed to be working in shifts to lend Scarlett a hand but more often than not they found themselves just sitting and watching the baby, unable to tear themselves away to do the more useful things that could help Scarlett. Right now they should be wrapping Holly and getting her ready for a sleep while Scarlett was in the shower but Ruby couldn't bring herself to relinquish her just yet. She was so delicate and perfect and Ruby could sit and hold her all day.

'What are your plans?' Lucy asked.

'Mum, do you mind if, for once, we don't have this conversation?'

'What do you mean?

'You always end up asking what my plans are. Making it sound as though I need to be settled down or have some grand vision for my future. I don't know what I'm doing.'

'But you've finished working for Noah. You must have some idea about what you're going to do next?'

And that was the crux of the matter. Noah didn't need her anymore.

Ruby tried counting to ten. She had tried to keep her New Year's resolution of being less argumentative but sometimes it was proving difficult. She knew she was on edge—she was missing Noah and that was making her more short-tempered than normal—but that wasn't

Lucy's fault and she shouldn't take it out on her, but she really didn't want to have this conversation. Again.

'I thought I might stay in Adelaide for a bit. I thought I'd stay to help Scarlett and to be here while Rose gets better.' Rose was recovering very slowly and at times Ruby felt as though she wasn't recovering at all. The infection had taken its toll on her kidneys and Rose now required dialysis. To add to that she needed surgery to amputate the tips of three of her toes. While it wasn't as bad as they had first feared, Ruby was still finding it confronting and staying for a while was an idea she'd had although she hadn't worked out the logistics. Things like where she would stay long term and how she would earn an income, all the things that Noah had worked out for her, were now her responsibility again.

'It would be lovely to have you home.'

Ruby wasn't sure if it was really what she wanted—in fact, she suspected it wasn't at all what she wanted—but she couldn't think of any other options right now. She heard the washing machine finish its final spin cycle and made her escape by offering to hang out the clothes.

The basket was half-empty when Scarlett joined her outside.

'Are you okay?'

'Why?'

'Mum thought she'd upset you.'

'Why can't she just accept that I don't have my life all mapped out?'

'I know you don't want to think you're like Mum but the truth is you are very similar—it's probably why you clash more with her than Rose or I do. But being like Mum isn't necessarily a bad thing. You are strong and independent—'

'I don't want to be independent,' Ruby said. 'I want Noah.'

'So what are you doing here? Why aren't you with him?'

'He doesn't need me anymore.'

'Has he said that?'

Ruby shook her head as she pegged a sock onto the line. 'No, but why would he? He's fine now. He'll be travelling around the country, doing what he does. I've got nowhere else I need to be so I thought I'd stay here.'

'What does he think you're doing here?'

'Helping you.'

'Did he ask you to go with him?'

'Yes.'

'But you chose to come here?'

'I didn't want to make the same mistakes Mum did.'

'What mistakes?'

'Falling for the wrong man.'

'Why is Noah the wrong man?'

Ruby had only intended to have some fun, as usual, but she was in over her head and afraid he would break her heart. 'Noah is in a completely different league from me. He flies around the country in private planes, stays in five-star penthouses and has a watch that is worth thousands of dollars.'

'None of those things are his. They're just perks of the job,' Scarlett pointed out.

'He still earns millions of dollars a year from his racing and sponsorships. He wears designer clothes and owns a beachfront house in Queensland. I shop at the markets or second-hand stores. When my things were packed up and sent over from Byron Bay they fitted into two moving boxes,' Ruby argued.

'So? Does that mean you don't deserve him?'

That was exactly how she felt. Because of her father's behaviour Ruby had never believed she was worthy of being loved. 'I was just the hired help.'

'Did he ever say that? Think of all the things Noah has done for you. He bought you a gorgeous dress that fitted you perfectly. I know he never asked for your size, he had paid enough attention to know. He has taken you to Sydney—twice. He has met all of us and even came to Christmas lunch when he could have insisted that you stay at the apartment with him. Does he even know you're not planning on coming back to him, that you're moving on from this relationship?'

'Not exactly.'

'You're doing it again, aren't you?'

'Doing what?'

'Running away. You need to ask yourself what you are running from.'

Ruby knew exactly why she was running.

'One day you have to stop running. You need to talk to Noah, you need to find out how he feels, you need to give him a chance. He should have a say in this. If you want what Jake and I have you can't keep pushing people away. One day you'll have to let someone in.'

But Ruby was terrified that once Noah knew all her secrets he wouldn't like her anymore. It was better just to leave and not find out.

But Scarlett hadn't finished. 'I know you don't want to be like Mum, and I know you're not going to like what I'm about to say, but I think you're showing more traits of your father.'

'What is that supposed to mean?'

'Running away. Not telling people how you really

feel. Mum has never hidden her feelings and she has faced up to her mistakes. She never did anything wrong except fall in love. It was our fathers who let her down. She has never let us down and neither have you. You can't be someone you're not and I'm sure Noah doesn't expect you to be, but don't you think he deserves to know who you are?'

Saturday, 28th February

He was back.

Ruby was by his side and her world felt infinitely better than it had three days ago.

She was standing on top of the pit building that had been erected for the V8 championship race. Noah stood behind her. His arms were wrapped around her waist and his lips brushed her ear and sent tingles through her as they surveyed the circuit. From the rooftop she could look across the park to the city.

The parklands and the streets on the eastern side of the city had been transformed. These were the same streets she'd been driving on, taking Noah to his appointments and visiting Rose in hospital but she wouldn't have recognised them. It looked like the circus had come to town, a massive, oversized circus.

Concrete barriers hemmed in the roads, turning them into a race track. Pedestrian bridges spanned the raceway and grandstands lined the circuit. Banners and flags waved in the breeze and added to the carnival atmosphere. There were vehicles everywhere—race cars, semi-trailers, news vans and food trucks. There was even a sideshow alley with showground rides and there were people everywhere.

Ruby couldn't believe the number of people who turned up to watch the races—hundreds of thousands over four days. Where had they all come from? It was busy and noisy and chaotic. Ruby's opinion had been that the race was for car fanatics but she suspected she would enjoy the spectacle too. It was crazy and colourful and loud and fun. And Noah was right there with her.

He'd been expecting to see her when he'd got back to Adelaide and she hadn't told him anything different. She had wanted to see him too. She hadn't even pretended to justify her behaviour to herself, she had run straight back to him as if her life depended on it. She had missed him and she had to admit that to herself, even if she wasn't prepared to admit it to anyone else. She had never felt like this about anyone.

She had been searching long and hard for her place to belong. She'd never expected to find it in the arms of a man. But she had to accept that she had found who and what she wanted in Noah. He was everything and all she wanted.

She had spent the past two days back in his arms and she never wanted to leave. She wondered if this was what being in love felt like.

'Come on,' he whispered. 'It's time to go.'

He needed to go and prepare for his race. Ruby had never watched a car race until today and she was extremely nervous when she thought of Noah out there among the action.

Noah left her with Ron Townsend, the team boss, in his corporate box. Ruby would have a good vantage point to watch the cars as they competed to see who could do the fastest lap and qualify for pole position on the grid for tomorrow's race.

The corporate box was in the pit building directly above the team's garages. Ruby kept her eyes peeled for car number twenty-two. There appeared to be no rigid system, it was all rather fluid. Cars would emerge from their garages and tear around the track in an attempt to post the fastest time before either retiring back into the garage or doing another lap. There was no lining up on the pit straight, no structure or fanfare. Rather the cars all seemed to do as they pleased.

Ruby held her breath when she saw Noah's car nose out of the garage. He merged into the traffic at the end of the pit lane.

'He'll have a lap to warm up his tyres first,' Ron explained, and Ruby relaxed and let out the breath.

Ron held a stopwatch in his hand. He turned his head to the left, waiting for Noah to reappear at the beginning of the pit straight.

Ruby saw Noah's car. He flew down the straight and in a matter of seconds had passed by them and was weaving through the chicane at the opposite end. Ron clicked his stopwatch as he went by.

'How fast do they go?' she asked.

'They can reach speeds of two hundred and sixty kilometres an hour.'

'What?' She had watched in the earlier races as cars had jostled for position, screaming around the circuit side by side, so close that several cars had had their side mirrors taken off by other competitors. Cars had spun or been shunted out of control and had collided with concrete walls, other cars and tyre barriers.

But the earlier races had just been a prelude for these cars. These were the cream of the crop and she could tell they were faster and would be more competitive. Being a spectator gave her quite an adrenalin rush and she could only imagine how Noah felt. She imagined it would be an addictive feeling. Battling to control the power of the engine in the hope of coming out victorious would surely put him on an adrenalin high.

Ron clicked the stopwatch as Noah came past again.

'Eighty-three seconds.'

'Is that good?'

'He'll need to shave a second or two off if he wants to qualify near the top of the list.'

'So they'll get their position on the grid and then come out tomorrow and do this for how many laps?'

'Seventy-eight.'

Ruby knew the race took about two hours to complete. She couldn't imagine keeping focused for that long at these sorts of speeds and especially not when there were twenty other cars on the track at the same time, all with the same goal—to cross the finish line in first place.

Watching the qualifying race clarified for her why he had spent so much time on his rehabilitation but she still found it difficult to comprehend that he'd made it back to the race track only eleven weeks after his accident. The G forces the drivers encountered, the effort required for the constant gear changes, not to mention the concentration required and the physical stress from the bumps from the track and the other cars, meant they needed to be super-fit.

The drivers' times were being displayed on the supersized television screens that were prominently positioned along the track. Ruby glanced up at Noah's time as he brought his car into the pit garage at the end of his third lap.

Jamie Winter in car number one had the time to beat. Eighty-one point six seconds.

Noah was currently tenth and Ruby wondered why he was coming in. Maybe he was happy with that position but qualifying didn't finish for another five minutes. What if someone else posted a faster time and pushed him down the rankings?

'Why isn't Noah out there?' she asked Ron.

'He'll wait until the last minute to try to post a faster lap. He'll be hoping that doesn't leave enough time for anyone else to catch him. This is a strategic competition. It's not just about who's the fastest, it's also about who plays the game the best.'

Ruby watched as the rankings on the screen were constantly updated as other cars finished and started their laps.

With three minutes to go, Noah came back onto the track. The first lap wasn't a complete lap, which meant he needed enough time to get around the circuit twice. Several other cars followed him out, including the current leader in car number one.

'Eighty-one point one seconds!' Ron clicked his stopwatch as Noah completed his final lap and Ruby waited for the time to be confirmed on the screen.

Noah had edged out Jamie Winter. He'd taken first place.

The clock counted down the seconds until the end of qualifying. With ten seconds remaining, Jamie's car crossed the start line.

'Damn.'

Ruby had one eye on the clock. 'He won't have time to finish his lap,' she said.

'It doesn't matter. As long as he starts it before the clock runs down he's allowed to finish.'

Ruby held her breath as she waited as one by one the last cars crossed the finish line.

Car number one turned the final corner.

Eighty-one point zero five seconds.

Noah had been squeezed out by the barest of margins.

Ron shrugged his shoulders. 'Can't complain about second fastest, it puts him on the front row,' was all he said, as he accompanied Ruby down to the pit garage.

Noah was out of the car. He had taken his helmet off and his hair was wet with perspiration. Ruby remembered him telling her the temperature in the cars could reach sixty degrees Celsius and she wondered how they tolerated that for an entire two-hour race.

Ruby hadn't seen him in his racing suit before. He looked fantastic—strong and capable.

It was red and white and fitted him like a second skin and she couldn't help but admire his bum as he bent over the engine to discuss something with one of the mechanics.

He straightened up, turned around and saw her. He was grinning from ear to ear. He pushed his hair off his forehead and tucked his helmet under his arm, reminding Ruby of her earliest fantasy involving Noah and a motorbike ride. She blushed just thinking about it.

He crossed the garage and scooped her up. 'I did it. I'm on the front row of the grid.'

Ruby knew how important it was to him to prove that he had made a full recovery and that the accident hadn't left him with any issues.

'What did you think?' he asked.

'It was incredible. Scary but incredible and you were amazing.'

He kissed her on the lips—she could taste the saltiness of his sweat but she wouldn't change a thing. He was pumped, on a massive high, and his enthusiasm was infectious. 'I'm going to get out of this suit. Come with me and you can tell me more about how amazing I was,' he said, still grinning widely as Ruby followed him out of the garage and into one of the team's semi-trailers that was parked behind the pit building.

The trucks were used to transport the cars, tyres and all the necessary equipment between circuits but during events the front half of the trailer was converted into a lounge for the drivers and the back half became a nerve centre and computer lab. The trailer was abandoned. They had it to themselves.

'So you enjoyed it, then?' he asked, as he ripped open the top of his racing jumpsuit. He had several layers of fireproof clothing underneath and he stripped these off too, leaving him standing semi-naked in front of her. He had been working hard to control his car as he'd sped around the circuit and the blood was still coursing through the muscles in his chest and arms. They were all clearly defined and as Ruby ran her eyes over his torso she thought he had never looked better.

'It was brilliant,' she said in a husky voice. 'There's a lot to like about motorsport.'

Ruby didn't know where all the other team members had gone and she didn't care. All she cared about was the fact that Noah was standing before her in a state of undress and she was as horny as it was humanly possible to be.

She stepped closer to him. 'Does the trailer have a lock?' she asked.

Noah didn't need to be asked twice. He slid the bolt across the door in one swift movement as Ruby ran her hands down his chest and into the back of his jumpsuit, pulling him hard against her. She tipped her head up, offering her lips to him, and he kissed her hard on her mouth.

Ruby pulled his jumpsuit a little lower, enough to free his erection. Noah started to help her to take it off but she stopped him. 'I want you to leave it on,' she told him. He was seriously sexy in this outfit.

Noah grinned and lifted Ruby off her feet. She wrapped her legs around his waist as she let him take control. For several weeks she had been the one in charge of their lovemaking. She had been restrained and cautious, conscious of the fact that his body was still healing. Now there were no such concerns and she could feel that Noah was eager to dictate the terms.

To her left a bench ran along the side wall of the trailer. Noah spun around ninety degrees and rested Ruby's butt on the edge of the bench. He let the bench take her weight, freeing his hands, and pushed her dress up to her waist. He pulled her knickers to one side; there was no time to remove them. Ruby heard the fabric rip but she was beyond caring. All she wanted was to feel Noah inside her.

Ruby clamped her legs tighter around his waist as he thrust inside her. She arched her back, wanting to take him as deep as she could, and cried out as she rode him. The adrenalin pumped through her veins and heightened her senses. The sex was frantic and urgent but no less enjoyable.

But she wanted time to remember every moment. Time to commit every touch to memory. She wanted to be able to recall how he tasted, how he looked and how he felt as he filled her.

She needed to make memories to store away for later. For when he left. His job was going to take him away from her.

All she would have left would be her memories.

Friday, 6th March

Noah had left for Melbourne. Ruby wanted to be there too.

He had asked her to go with him but she couldn't be in two places at once. Rose and her family needed her here and she had made a choice, a responsible, grown-up adult choice, where she did the right thing by others, rather than just choosing whatever suited her. She knew she'd made the right choice but it was tough.

Rose needed a kidney transplant. The bacteria had irreparably damaged her kidneys and the dialysis wasn't going to be a long-term option.

Rose needed her family around her. Rose needed her more than Noah did so Ruby had stayed. She was undergoing tests to see if she was a compatible donor. Her blood type was compatible but that was only step one. She had undergone several tests already and was waiting on the first lot of results.

The transplant team had done a skin cross-match, which had involved taking a small sample of skin from under her arm and incubating these cells in Rose's serum to see if they survived or were destroyed.

Noah knew she was expecting the first lot of test results. He phoned her before his race but unfortunately this was only minutes after the doctors had called her with the news that she was incompatible. Her skin cells had been destroyed. Her kidney was not an option for Rose.

She was devastated and felt lost.

She hadn't intended to watch the race. She needed to start putting some distance between her and Noah if she was going to be able to let go and move on, but she couldn't resist. She needed to see him. And seeing him on television was as close as she was going to get.

Ruby turned the television on just as the cars were lining up on the grid. Subconsciously she'd known exactly when the race was due to start.

It was only an exhibition race, there were no championship points being awarded, but that didn't stop the competitiveness of the drivers.

Noah was starting from third position. At the very first corner his car was clipped by the car behind. Ruby watched, horrified, as the impact turned Noah ninety degrees before the car behind slammed into his passenger door, pushing him sideways along the track. His car collided with the kerbing and rolled, doing a full somersault across the track.

Ruby's heart was pounding as she watched his car flip a second time and collide, midway through the flip, at high speed with the tyre wall. His car was tossed into the air and came to land with a sickening thud on its roof.

The windscreen exploded, sending fragments of safety glass across the track, and the front of the car was completely crushed.

Ruby was stunned. She couldn't bear to watch as the television network showed the crash over and over again but she couldn't make herself move. Her body and her brain had shut down, refusing to believe what she was seeing.

But she was seeing it again and again—in slow motion, in real time and from all different angles. She managed to mute the sound but she couldn't bring herself to change the channel or switch the television off. She needed to keep watching. She had to know what had happened to Noah.

Was he okay? Was he hurt? Was he still alive?

She eventually realised she needed to hear the commentary if she wanted to know anything. She turned the sound back on as the vision showed the safety car out on the track. An ambulance was pulling up on the other side of the concrete barrier and a tow truck was angled across the road.

And then she saw him.

He was climbing out of the car. Out through a window.

She let out the breath she hadn't been aware of holding as she saw him pull himself out through the side window. He was okay.

But just as she thought that his knees buckled and she watched helplessly as he collapsed onto the track. The paramedics were quick to get to him and the last thing Ruby saw was Noah being bundled into the back of the ambulance.

She turned the television off as the ambulance drove away with its lights flashing.

She didn't know what to do. She didn't know what she *could* do.

Her first instinct was to run to Noah. But he was close to eight hundred kilometres away in Melbourne and there were people here who needed her too. Rose's condition was worsening and baby Holly wasn't feeding properly because Scarlett was stressed. They need her too but who needed her most? All she could think about was Noah.

What if he wasn't okay? What would she do?

Ruby felt like she should now be in three places at once. With Rose, with Scarlett and with Noah. She wished someone would tell her where to go or what to do.

It was too much for her to handle and her first impulse was to run away, but she had promised Scarlett she'd try to resist that impulse.

But her promises mean nothing.

She still wanted to run. She just didn't know in which direction to go.

CHAPTER TEN

NOAH WAS IRRITABLE but it had nothing to do with the accident. Unfortunately for him, his out-of-character irritability was attributed to a suspected second concussion, which only served to increase his irritability as he was forced to follow routine medical procedure.

Despite what the medicos thought, he *knew* he didn't have concussion. He'd tried to tell the doctors at the track that but no one had been listening. He'd tried to talk his way out of a trip to the hospital but the medicos hadn't been prepared to take a chance—in their opinion, today's accident and possible repercussions were too close to his earlier crash and they weren't about to take his word for it. He'd been carted off to hospital and now he was cooling his heels, waiting for the results of a brain scan.

All the other tests had been normal and he was becoming increasingly frustrated as more time passed. He wasn't normally an impatient man but there were other things he wanted to be doing.

He kept one eye on the clock as the hospital staff kept one eye on him. He knew they were watching him like hawks—if they hadn't been paying such close attention he would have made a break for it. He needed to get to a phone.

Finally the doctor arrived with the verdict—all clear. No surprises there.

What a waste of time.

Noah didn't waste any more of it. He made a dash for a hospital phone. He dialled Ruby's number, knowing she would be worried about him. His phone was back at the race track—which was just as well. He could only imagine what the nurses would have said if he'd pulled his mobile phone out to make a call while he'd been in Emergency.

His call went straight to her message service.

He left a message, thinking she must be on the phone, and after signing his discharge papers he tried again.

And he tried a third time while he waited for a ride back to the circuit. But each time he got her message service.

That was odd. He'd assumed she'd be waiting for a call from him.

He wondered what was going on but he had no way of finding out. He could remember no other numbers. Maybe the accident had rattled him more than he'd thought.

He checked his phone the moment he got back to the track but there was no message from Ruby. No missed calls. Nothing. It had been almost three hours since his accident—why couldn't he contact her?

Scarlett's home number was in his phone. He had no other choice. He had to find Ruby. He dialled Scarlett.

'Scarlett, it's Noah—'

'Noah! Are you okay? Is everything all right?'

'Yes, I'm fine. I'm trying to get hold of Ruby but she's not answering her phone. Do you know where she is?'

'She's not with you?'

'No. Should she be?' He frowned. Had he missed something? Forgotten something? He was starting to think he had suffered another bump to the head.

'She saw your accident on television. She told me she was flying to Melbourne to see you. You haven't heard from her?'

'No, her phone is switched off.'

'Maybe she's on the plane.'

He couldn't understand why she hadn't called and left him a message. Maybe she'd panicked. 'Did she tell you what airline she was going to fly with?'

'No. She was going to the airport to get on the next available flight.'

He could tell Scarlett was worried now. He was too. He took a deep breath as he tried to calm his nerves and settle Scarlett's at the same time. 'I'll call the airlines and get flight details, see if I can work out which flight she's on. I'll let you know as soon as I hear anything.'

He paced up and down inside the trailer while he made calls. The first two airlines he rang both had flights that Ruby could have been on but both had already landed in Melbourne and he still hadn't heard from her. He couldn't sit and wait, he was too restless, too worried. Something didn't feel right.

He called in a favour and got a lift to the airport. He'd wait for her there. He wanted to be on hand when she landed.

But two hours later he'd still heard nothing. Ruby was still out of contact. She hadn't miraculously appeared in Melbourne and Scarlett had heard nothing either.

Now he was really worried. He knew she was stressed about Rose. What had she done? Where was she?

Something was wrong. He could feel it in his gut. It

was twisting and churning and making him feel quite nauseous. He'd waited long enough. He would have to go and find her.

His mind flashed back to the last time he'd waited.

Ten years ago he'd waited for his brother to come home. Ten years ago he'd waited too long. He wasn't going to make the same mistake twice.

He jumped on the next available flight to Adelaide and checked his phone the minute he was allowed to switch it on. Still nothing.

He hurried along the concourse with little idea of what he was going to do or where he was heading.

He called Scarlett. 'I'm here. Have you heard anything?'

'No.'

By now no one had seen or heard from Ruby for several hours. He knew she'd run away before—she'd run away to Melbourne when she was sixteen, she'd run away with him to be his carer rather than stay with her mother, and she'd run from him when he'd wanted to take her to meet his parents. It seemed whenever she was under stress she took flight. The difference this time was no one knew where she'd gone.

He had to find her.

'What do I do?' he asked Scarlett. He wasn't used to being uncertain. He was good at making decisions. In his job he often had to make quick, life-or-death decisions and he knew that wasting time in second-guessing himself was futile. But motor racing was different, he'd had experience in those situations. He'd had plenty of practice behind the wheel of a racing car but his feelings for Ruby were a whole different ballgame and he was terrified that something had happened. Something *must* have happened for her to disappear off the radar like this.

Despite all the time they'd spent together, there was still so much he had to learn about her. But he did know that this was out of character, even for her. He couldn't imagine her disappearing without telling Scarlett. She'd told her she was getting on a plane and maybe she had, but she hadn't flown to Melbourne. How on earth was he going to find her?

What did he know? Where might she go? And then it hit him and he knew exactly where Ruby would be. Her safe place.

The palm house.

He couldn't believe he hadn't thought of it before. He looked at his watch, the designer watch that Ruby had teased him about. What time did the gardens close? It was already five o'clock.

'Noah, are you there?'

Scarlett's voice interrupted his thoughts. He'd almost forgotten she was on the other end of the phone.

'Yes, I'm still here.'

'I said come to my house. Jake will be home soon, he can go with you to start looking.'

'No. I need to go to the botanic gardens,' Noah said.

'What on earth for?'

'She took me to a place there once. She might have gone back there.'

'I don't think that's where she'll be.'

There was a pause as Noah waited for Scarlett to elaborate but she didn't continue.

'Scarlett? You're worrying me. Do you know where to find her? You don't think she would have done any-thing silly, do you?' He'd already lost his brother and he refused to accept that he couldn't save Ruby. He couldn't lose her too.

'Nothing we shouldn't be able to undo.'

'What does that mean?'

'You need to start looking in bars, in hotels.'

'Bars? Why?' Nothing was making much sense. He was struggling to get things straight in his head. 'Ruby doesn't drink.'

'Has she told you why?'

'She told me she doesn't like the way it makes her feel.'

'It's a bit more complicated than that. It's really her story to tell but I'm worried that the stress of recent events—Rose's condition and now your accident—might have pushed her over the edge. We'll have to start looking somewhere and the bars and pubs is my guess. I'll meet you at my house and we can work out where to start.'

He couldn't imagine his life without Ruby in it. In a matter of weeks she had become a part of him, a part that he couldn't do without. He had fallen in love with her. He needed to find her and tell her.

He didn't care what she was doing as long as he found her, and he was positive Scarlett was wrong.

He was sure he knew where she'd be.

'I'm going to the botanic gardens. I'll call you when I find her.'

He disconnected the call and headed for the exit. His path took him past one of the airport bars. He glanced inside, not expecting to see anyone he knew, but Scarlett's words were ringing in his head. A girl with red hair was sitting at the bar. He hesitated and took a second look. Did she resemble Ruby because he wanted her to?

The bar was dimly lit, making it difficult to see for sure. He walked in. He didn't want to find her in here. He didn't want Scarlett to be right.

'Ruby?'

The girl turned and lifted her head. She was a stranger.

Noah kept going, cursing himself for wasting time. He hailed a taxi and promised the driver he'd double his fare if he got him there in under half an hour. He couldn't risk the chance that the gardens would be closed.

He sprinted through the park, cutting across the lawn as he made a beeline for the palm house. The late afternoon sun was shining on the glass, turning it into one giant mirror. He held his hand up against the glare as he raced up the front steps, taking them three at a time and not stopping until he was in the centre of the building. He looked up and down the pathway as he called her name.

'Ruby?'

'Noah!' She was down the pathway to his right. 'You're all right!' She jumped up from the wall and ran towards him. Her eyes were red, she'd obviously been crying, but her face lit up and she managed a smile for him.

'I'm fine,' he said. 'What are you doing here?' he asked as he wrapped her in his arms. She felt so good. This was where she belonged. With him.

'I had some things to think about.'

'I've been calling you for hours. Why didn't you answer?'

'I left my phone at Scarlett's. The battery was flat.'

'How long have you been here?'

'I have no idea.' She paused, thinking. 'I saw the accident on television,' she added. 'How long ago was that?'

'Almost seven hours ago.'

'I guess I've been here for a few hours, then.'

Ruby wasn't sure where that time had gone. Her first
instinct when she'd seen the accident had been to run
to Noah and she'd even told Scarlett that was what she
planned to do, but she hadn't been able to make herself
go through with it. She hadn't thought she could bear
to be rejected. It had been a stressful day—finding out
she was an incompatible donor for Rose and then seeing
Noah's horrific accident had almost been too much for
her to handle. She couldn't stand the thought of something happening to either Noah or Rose. She hadn't
wanted to consider that one day they might not be
around but that was the possibility she'd faced today.
She couldn't afford to take them for granted. One day
they might not be there.

She'd felt so helpless watching Noah's accident and
she couldn't stand to think that she could lose him.

She would give anything to keep him safe.

She loved him.

She recognised the feeling now. She was in love.

It was time to stop being afraid of letting people into
her life. It was time to let people close but she didn't
know how to do that.

She'd needed some space. She'd needed time to think
about what this all meant and what she was going to do.
And that had been when she'd headed to the palm house.

The palm house was her sanctuary. But it wasn't
where she wanted to be. Not today.

She wanted to stop running but she didn't think she
was brave enough. It had been a promise she'd made to

herself twelve weeks ago but it was something she was struggling with.

The palm house had always given her hope that one day she'd find a place where she belonged. And she'd found it. Only it wasn't a place. It was Noah.

Noah was her palm house. She belonged with him.

'It's time to go.' Noah unwrapped her from his embrace and took her hand.

Ruby shook her head. 'I think I might stay.' She needed Noah to say he wanted her to go with him. If he didn't, she may as well stay put. She sat down on the retaining wall.

'You can't stay here,' Noah said. 'The park is closing soon and I'm not leaving here without you.'

'You'll have to leave eventually,' she replied. 'You'll have to go back to Melbourne. The races aren't over.'

'They're over for me.'

'You did get hurt!' Ruby ran her eyes over him, searching for injuries, but he looked unscathed.

He was shaking his head. 'I'm fine but you are far more important and you are coming with me. Let me look after you.'

She gave in because she was too tired to argue. And because she'd wanted Noah to take charge of the situation and look after her.

He had booked them into a hotel on the beachfront at Glenelg. They had nowhere else to go but Ruby didn't care where she was as long as she was with him. He ordered room service while she had a shower. They were both exhausted.

Their corner suite overlooked the beach and Noah had turned the couch around so they were nestled into the bay window. Ruby was curled up into the curve of his side, watching a summer lightning storm light up the sky. There was no rain but the air sparked with electricity as the lightning forks hit the ocean.

Watching the lightning hit the water was reminiscent of the impact Noah had had on her. She was the water and his touch was the lightning that turned her to steam.

'You told Scarlett you were coming to me. Why didn't you?' His voice was deep in his chest, rumbling like the distant thunder.

'I couldn't decide if that was the right decision. I was scared.'

'Of what?'

'I have never run towards someone before. I've always run away.' Her first response had always been flight. She might have deliberated that point with Scarlett but she knew it was true.

'Why?'

'When the going gets tough,' Ruby said, 'the tough get going.'

'It doesn't mean they run away. It means they get ready to fight for what they want,' Noah told her. 'I'm in your corner. I will fight with you and for you.'

'You might not say that if you knew the real me. There are a lot of things you don't know.'

'If there are, it's only because you haven't told me. Why haven't you let me in?' he asked.

'I don't like it when people get too close.'

'Why not?'

'If they get close they can hurt me.'

'How?'

'By getting to know the real me,' she finally admitted. 'I've done some things I'm not proud of.'

'That's the beauty of life, though—if you're lucky you

get a chance to fix your mistakes. You get a chance to make amends. I think you're special and I can't imagine there is anything you could tell me that would change my mind.'

'I'm not so sure about that.'

'Why don't you try me?'

Ruby closed her eyes and tucked herself closer against Noah's chest. It was time to stop being afraid. It was time to let him into her life, and if she was going to do that he needed to hear her story.

She felt safe with him, she'd felt like that since the day she'd met him, and she just hoped she was right in thinking she could trust him. To tell him her whole story would be like entrusting him with her soul.

She took a deep breath and began.

'I was a bit of a difficult teenager. Mum and I clashed constantly. Rose's dad had died and Mum was struggling to keep me under control. When I was sixteen I decided I'd had enough of Mum telling me what to do and I ran off to Melbourne to live with my father. A man who I'd never met and who I found out wanted nothing to do with me.

'The whole thing was an absolute disaster but I was too proud to admit my mistake and go home. I knew my "father" wouldn't tell Mum what was going on so I stayed in Melbourne, with a man who didn't want me around and who couldn't care less about what I got up to. So of course I got up to lots of things that no sixteen-year-old should.

'I dropped out of school and proceeded to get deeper and deeper into trouble. I was drinking a lot and one day I woke up in a strange bed. I had no idea where I was or what I'd been doing.'

'Where were your friends?

'I didn't have friends. Acquaintances maybe, for want of a better word, but no one who had the maturity or the empathy to watch out for another kid or to stop me from getting into trouble. If anything, they contributed to the problem.'

'What about your family? Your mum? Scarlett?'

'They were in Adelaide. They didn't know what I was up to.'

'A few weeks later I found out I was pregnant. I was terrified. I couldn't go home to Mum—I realise now that of course I could have, but at the time I didn't think it was an option. Mum had Scarlett when she was eighteen and one of the things Mum and I argued about was that I didn't want to be like her. And falling pregnant at seventeen was history repeating itself. I'd been drinking a lot and I was terrified I'd hurt the baby. I had no idea who the father was and I was not emotionally capable of being a mother. I didn't know what to do.'

'What happened?'

'I had a miscarriage. I think my body was in no condition to be pregnant and it was probably the best outcome but I've felt guilty ever since. But it had happened and I couldn't change it. All I could do was change my behaviour. I stopped drinking after that and I haven't had a drink since. I have never been good at dealing with conflict or resolving problems. I've always opted to run away to avoid dealing with anything unpleasant or stressful and back then I escaped by abusing alcohol.'

'You obviously survived and came through this. How did you do that?'

'Scarlett. She figured out something was wrong. She

came to Melbourne and got me sorted. She got me to go back to school and got me out of trouble.'

'You must have some inner strength of your own too.'

'Why do you say that?' Ruby lifted her head and opened her eyes. She needed to see him.

'I imagine you've been under considerable pressure with Rose's illness and I assume today was stressful for you yet you got yourself through it. I think you are stronger than you give yourself credit for.'

'I barely got through today. I was just hoping that if I pretended everything was fine, maybe it would be. I've always done that. But today it wasn't working. There was too much to ignore. Rose's illness, Scarlett and the baby and you.'

'Me? What about me?'

'I'm a bit overwhelmed by how you make me feel. You make me feel like I did when I was drinking and that scares me.'

'I don't understand.'

'I liked the way I felt about the world, about myself, more after a few drinks. I wanted to feel better about myself and drinking helped me do that. Then it got to the point where I needed a drink. And then more than one.

'I felt the same way about you. I feel better about myself when I am with you but I don't want to be dependent on someone else for that. But I'm afraid that is what will happen. I'm afraid I won't be able to give you up.

'I'm not the same person I was ten years ago. But I'm still trying to find out who I am exactly and where I belong. Ten years ago I was searching for myself as much as I was looking for a place to belong. I didn't like the person I became when I was in Melbourne but without Scarlett's help I don't think I would have made it. Sometimes I still feel the same way. That I'm searching and searching but I haven't found what I'm looking for. I keep thinking that if I find somewhere I feel comfortable I'll be able to find the real me. But I've realised it's not a place I've been searching for.

'When I watched you in that accident today I felt as though it was me in that car. It felt like my heart was getting ripped apart but all I cared about was whether or not you were going to be okay. Nothing else mattered. Only you. I haven't been searching for a place, I've been searching for a person. I've been searching for you.'

'Why didn't you get on a plane and come to me?'

'Because I wasn't brave enough. I didn't know if you felt the same way and I wasn't sure if I was strong enough to cope if you didn't want me. You needed me when you were injured but you're not injured now and I don't know where that leaves me.'

'I want you with me. What will it take to get you to run to me instead of away?'

'I need to know you'll be there for me no matter what.'

'How can I prove that to you except with time?'

'You could tell me about your ex-wife.'

'Steph? Why?'

'I want to know what happened between you. I need to know that you tried to make it work. I need to know you're not going to give up on me.'

'Why would I give up on you?'

'Because I might not be what you expect.'

'No one expects you to be someone you're not. Being someone others expect you to be isn't sustainable. You have to be the person you are meant to be. I know because I tried to change for Steph. I wasn't coping at all with Adam's suicide. Getting married was Steph's idea, she thought it would fix me, make me happy again. I figured I didn't have anything to lose, things couldn't get worse, so I agreed.

'There were some parts of me that I wanted to change but I didn't want to give up my dream of racing cars. That was the only thing that made me feel better. So I kept my contract and got promoted up the ranks until I spent most of the year away, driving. That wasn't what Steph had had in mind. She didn't like travelling all the time and she didn't like being left alone. There was no easy solution to that dilemma so we split. But I liked being married. I liked the companionship, I believe in the commitment but we couldn't make it work. We didn't have the same dream and in the end I couldn't be the person she wanted me to be.

'And that's why I don't expect you to be someone you're not. I love you just the way you are.'

'You love me?'

'I do. You are kind, funny, considerate, adorable, sexy and strong and I'm not complete without you. I need you. All I could think about when I was being carted off to hospital was you. And when I couldn't find you I was going crazy. I was terrified that something had happened to you. I didn't know how I would survive that. I don't want to be in a world without you and I promise that if you'll have me, I will never leave you. I want to share my life with you. I didn't know you ten years ago but I know you now and I love you, just the way you are.' He paused then added, 'Except for maybe one small thing.'

'What is it?' she asked, not really sure if she wanted to hear the answer.

'I want you to have a husband.'

'A husband?'

Noah nodded as he unwrapped his arm from around her shoulders and got down on one knee. 'Ruby, will you marry me?'

'Yes,' she said, as she laughed and pulled him to his feet.

'Yes,' she repeated, as she stood up and stepped into his embrace.

'Yes,' she said, as she kissed him.

'I love you, too,' she said, as another lightning fork split the sky. But she was oblivious to the storm, she wasn't aware of anything other than Noah. She was in his arms. She was right where she belonged. She'd made it.

* * * * *

Mills & Boon® Hardback
November 2014

ROMANCE

A Virgin for His Prize	Lucy Monroe
The Valquez Seduction	Melanie Milburne
Protecting the Desert Princess	Carol Marinelli
One Night with Morelli	Kim Lawrence
To Defy a Sheikh	Maisey Yates
The Russian's Acquisition	Dani Collins
The True King of Dahaar	Tara Pammi
Rebel's Bargain	Annie West
The Million-Dollar Question	Kimberly Lang
Enemies with Benefits	Louisa George
Man vs. Socialite	Charlotte Phillips
Fired by Her Fling	Christy McKellen
The Twelve Dates of Christmas	Susan Meier
At the Chateau for Christmas	Rebecca Winters
A Very Special Holiday Gift	Barbara Hannay
A New Year Marriage Proposal	Kate Hardy
A Little Christmas Magic	Alison Roberts
Christmas with the Maverick Millionaire	Scarlet Wilson

MEDICAL

Playing the Playboy's Sweetheart	Carol Marinelli
Unwrapping Her Italian Doc	Carol Marinelli
A Doctor by Day...	Emily Forbes
Tamed by the Renegade	Emily Forbes

ROMANCE

Christakis's Rebellious Wife	Lynne Graham
At No Man's Command	Melanie Milburne
Carrying the Sheikh's Heir	Lynn Raye Harris
Bound by the Italian's Contract	Janette Kenny
Dante's Unexpected Legacy	Catherine George
A Deal with Demakis	Tara Pammi
The Ultimate Playboy	Maya Blake
Her Irresistible Protector	Michelle Douglas
The Maverick Millionaire	Alison Roberts
The Return of the Rebel	Jennifer Faye
The Tycoon and the Wedding Planner	Kandy Shepherd

HISTORICAL

A Lady of Notoriety	Diane Gaston
The Scarlet Gown	Sarah Mallory
Safe in the Earl's Arms	Liz Tyner
Betrayed, Betrothed and Bedded	Juliet Landon
Castle of the Wolf	Margaret Moore

MEDICAL

200 Harley Street: The Proud Italian	Alison Roberts
200 Harley Street: American Surgeon in London	Lynne Marshall
A Mother's Secret	Scarlet Wilson
Return of Dr Maguire	Judy Campbell
Saving His Little Miracle	Jennifer Taylor
Heatherdale's Shy Nurse	Abigail Gordon

Mills & Boon® Hardback
December 2014

ROMANCE

Taken Over by the Billionaire	Miranda Lee
Christmas in Da Conti's Bed	Sharon Kendrick
His for Revenge	Caitlin Crews
A Rule Worth Breaking	Maggie Cox
What The Greek Wants Most	Maya Blake
The Magnate's Manifesto	Jennifer Hayward
To Claim His Heir by Christmas	Victoria Parker
Heiress's Defiance	Lynn Raye Harris
Nine Month Countdown	Leah Ashton
Bridesmaid with Attitude	Christy McKellen
An Offer She Can't Refuse	Shoma Narayanan
Breaking the Boss's Rules	Nina Milne
Snowbound Surprise for the Billionaire	Michelle Douglas
Christmas Where They Belong	Marion Lennox
Meet Me Under the Mistletoe	Cara Colter
A Diamond in Her Stocking	Kandy Shepherd
Falling for Dr December	Susanne Hampton
Snowbound with the Surgeon	Annie Claydon

MEDICAL

Midwife's Christmas Proposal	Fiona McArthur
Midwife's Mistletoe Baby	Fiona McArthur
A Baby on Her Christmas List	Louisa George
A Family This Christmas	Sue MacKay

Mills & Boon® Large Print

December 2014

ROMANCE

Zarif's Convenient Queen	Lynne Graham
Uncovering Her Nine Month Secret	Jennie Lucas
His Forbidden Diamond	Susan Stephens
Undone by the Sultan's Touch	Caitlin Crews
The Argentinian's Demand	Cathy Williams
Taming the Notorious Sicilian	Michelle Smart
The Ultimate Seduction	Dani Collins
The Rebel and the Heiress	Michelle Douglas
Not Just a Convenient Marriage	Lucy Gordon
A Groom Worth Waiting For	Sophie Pembroke
Crown Prince, Pregnant Bride	Kate Hardy

HISTORICAL

Beguiled by Her Betrayer	Louise Allen
The Rake's Ruined Lady	Mary Brendan
The Viscount's Frozen Heart	Elizabeth Beacon
Mary and the Marquis	Janice Preston
Templar Knight, Forbidden Bride	Lynna Banning

MEDICAL

200 Harley Street: The Soldier Prince	Kate Hardy
200 Harley Street: The Enigmatic Surgeon	Annie Claydon
A Father for Her Baby	Sue MacKay
The Midwife's Son	Sue MacKay
Back in Her Husband's Arms	Susanne Hampton
Wedding at Sunday Creek	Leah Martyn

MILLS & BOON®

Why shop at millsandboon.co.uk?

Each year, thousands of romance readers find their perfect read at millsandboon.co.uk. That's because we're passionate about bringing you the very best romantic fiction. Here are some of the advantages of shopping at www.millsandboon.co.uk:

* **Get new books first**—you'll be able to buy your favourite books one month before they hit the shops

* **Get exclusive discounts**—you'll also be able to buy our specially created monthly collections, with up to 50% off the RRP

* **Find your favourite authors**—latest news, interviews and new releases for all your favourite authors and series on our website, plus ideas for what to try next

* **Join in**—once you've bought your favourite books, don't forget to register with us to rate, review and join in the discussions

Visit **www.millsandboon.co.uk**
for all this and more today!